Seven Oaks

Murray Pura

For JRD
who, 150 years later, is a niece of Stonewall Jackson –
all the best to you
thank you!

Copyright 2014 Murray Pura ©

This book is a work of fiction. The names, characters, places, and incidents are products of the writer's imagination or have been used fictitiously and are not to be construed as real. Any resemblance to persons, living or dead, actual events, locales or organizations is purely coincidental.

All rights reserved. The author guarantees all contents are original and do not infringe upon the legal rights of any other person or work. No part of this book may be used or reproduced, stored in a retrieval system or transmitted in any form or by any means without prior written permission of the publisher, except in the case of brief quotations embodied in critical articles and reviews.

The views and opinions expressed in this book may not be those of the publisher.

First Edition

Published by

Helping Hands Press

ISBN: 9781622085262

Printed in the United States of America

Other titles by Murray Pura

The Rose of Saratoga County
　　Volume 1 – The Thirteen Colonies

The Rose of Lancaster County:
　　Volume 1 - The Rose Garden
　　Volume 2 - The Covenant
　　Volume 3 - The First Frost
　　Volume 4 - A Rose Among Thorns
　　Volume 5 - The Trial
　　Volume 6 - The Kiss
　　Volume 7 - A Rose in Winter
　　Volume 8 - Resurrection
　　Volume 9 - The Execution
　　Volume 10 - The Wedding Quilt
　　The Complete eBook

Remington Colt's Revolutionary War Series - The Declaration of Independence
　　Volume 1 - Thomas Jefferson

Preacher Man
　　Volume 1 – The Devil to Pay

American Civil War Series - Cry of Freedom:
　　Volume 1 - Return To Shirley Plantation
　　Volume 2 - The Last Waltz
　　Volume 3 - Bachelor Buttons
　　Volume 4 - Olivia's Wedding
　　Volume 6 - Gettysburg's Chosen Sons
　　Volume 7 - Sheltering Arms
　　Volume 8 - Safe House
　　Volume 9 - A Gettysburg Vignette [
　　Volume 10 - To Paint a Sunrise
　　Volume 11 - Sweet Child of Mine
　　Volume 12 - Kentucky Rain
　　Volume 13 - Soldier's Heart
　　Volume 14 - Black Rain
　　Volume 15 - The Star

The Name of The Hawk series:
　　Volume 1 - Legion
　　Volume 2 - The Land Beyond The Stars
　　Volume 3 – Flame

The Painted Sky:
- Volume 1 - Rio Oro
- Volume 2 - The Widow & the Preacher
- Volume 3 - The Australian Way
- Volume 4 - A Church Called Lazarus
- Volume 5 - The Fight
- Volume 6 – Betrayal
- Volume 7 - The Shadow of the Almighty
- Volume 8 - All the Colors of Heaven
- The Complete eBook

The Blue Heaven Romance Series:
- Volume 1 - Emalyn's Treasure
- Volume 2 - Blister Creek
- Volume 3 - Do No Harm
- Volume 4 - Heaven Is Not Far
- Volume 5 - The Whispers of Angels
- Volume 6 - A Dragon's Kiss
- Volume 7 - The Bar Maid of Dodge City
- Volume 8 - Jolly Angel
- Volume 9 - Love's Eternal Flame

The Wells Fargo Express Series
- Remington Colt - Volume 1 - The Desperate Road

Seven Oaks:
- Volume 1 - The Plantation
- Volume 2 - Stonewall
- Volume 3 - The Storm
- Volume 4 - Firebrand
- Volume 5 - A Wedding In Virginia
- Volume 6 - Raindrops
- Volume 7 - A Seven Oaks Christmas
- The Complete eBook

Marsha Hubler's Heart-Warming Horse Stories
- Volume One - All the Pretty Little Ponies

Streams: Seeking God in the Waters of Scripture

Rooted: Finding God in the Gardens of Scripture

Mark Miller's One 2013
- Volume 5 - White Man's God

Connect with Murray:
www.murraypura.com

The Plantation

1852

"Sarah! Sarah Nunley!"

The nine year old girl with golden brown eyes and long brown hair crouched behind a huge oak tree and said nothing as the tall black man made his way through the ferns and undergrowth of the forest.

"Miss Sarah! Now I know you're down here somewheres. Speak up. Don't make it hard on Billy King." The man peered at the numerous trees and bushes. "It's not about schooling or your lessons. Your Uncle Thomas has come to pay you a visit. You hear me? Uncle Thomas has come up from Lexington and left his teaching work at the Institute just to see you."

Sarah sprang out from behind the tree. "What did you say, Billy?"

The man tried to look annoyed at the slim girl in the yellow dress but gave it up and broke into a smile. "You are just like some kind of brown fox sneaking around here in the woods. You watch or some hunter is gonna snare you."

"I'm too quick for any hunter hereabouts, Billy." She ran up to him and took his hand. "Where is Uncle Thomas?"

"Up at the house with your father and mother. Come on."

"Is he in his blue uniform from the school?"

"Yes, he is, Miss Sarah."

"With a sword?"

"Yes."

She skipped as she held Billy's hand. "Oh, he must look so dashing."

The man laughed. "I can't tell you anything about that. It's for you to say."

"Or for his lady to say. He doesn't have a lady yet, does he, Billy?"

"Not so far as I knows."

"Good."

An acorn bounced off the top of her head.

"Ouch." She put a hand on the spot. "Who did that?"

Another acorn struck her shoulder.

"Hey!" Her face became a crisscross of lines. "It's my brother Warren, that pest!"

Billy grinned and ducked as more acorns came their way. "I don't expect. He's at his Latin. Ask yourself, Miss Sarah, who's the artilleryman in the family?"

"Why – " She put her hands on her hips. "Thomas J. Jackson! Shame on you for firing at civilians! I thought you were a Southern gentleman!"

A head popped up from a thick bush. "I wasn't truly firing at you, Sarah. Just sending round shot your way to get your attention."

"Get my attention? You hit me twice!"

"Sometimes the fortunes of war blow ill."

"If I had my own acorns I would return fire."

"Well, it's September and they are all around. Mind you don't soil your dress or your hands."

Sarah ran towards him. "You have your fancy uniform on. With your sword."

"Fancy?" Blue eyes glittered. "There's nothing fancy about this uniform. It's just plain and well-tailored and comfortable."

"And the sword is for beheading students?"

"That's right. Any cadet who doesn't do well on exams."

She smiled as she tugged at one of the brass buttons sewn in a double row on the front of the blue frock coat. "You promised me one of these buttons for a souvenir."

He scooped her up. "I did but not off my school uniform. I have to teach in this one."

"I always forget the name for what you teach, uncle." She put her slim arms about his neck. "It's too long a title."

"Professor of Natural and Experimental Philosophy."

"And?"

"And Instructor of Artillery. Mind you don't forget anymore."

She laughed. "Such big words. How does all you do go together, Uncle Thomas?"

"It goes together very well. You must keep your thinking in proper alignment and once you do it all fits." He smiled at Billy King.

"Thank you for being my scout. You may return to the tasks your master has set for you."

"Yes, sir."

Sarah kissed her uncle's cheek. "Your beard looks well."

"Thank you for saying so."

"Do you have a lady yet?"

"Not yet."

"But you are quite old. Soon you'll be passed the marrying age."

"I'm only twenty-eight, Sarah, not fifty-eight."

She stroked the beard with her little girl fingers. "You're so old you might as well wait and marry me. I'll be fifteen in six years. I can be your bride in white silk before you know it."

"Fifteen?"

"Mom was only a little older than that."

"I don't think Southern gentlemen marry their nieces. Not even favorite ones."

"Why not?" Sarah pouted. "Is there a law against it in Virginia?"

"There probably is a law. And another one in the Bible." He continued to carry her through the woods. "Where were you hiding?"

She pointed. "There."

"Good choice. No wonder Billy couldn't find you. One of the seven oaks, eh? Big around as four or five cannon."

"Let's play *raindrops*."

"*Raindrops?*"

"Yes, it's been such a long time and I know you'll be gone after this and teaching until Christmas."

"Well." Uncle Thomas set her down on her feet. "There hadn't been rain in the land of Israel for more than three years because of the sins of its people and the evil of its rulers. But Elijah the prophet made war against the men who enslaved his country. He called down fire from the heavens and had the wicked priests of Baal slain."

"But not the king."

"No, not the king. That was for God to do if he so wished. Not Elijah."

He settled down in the soft grass under one of the oak trees and Sarah sat in his lap. She took his blue forage cap from his head and held it.

"So Elijah told King Ahab he could hear the sound of heavy rain. It wasn't raining but God put the sound in his head. He knew it was going to come. He advised the king to get something to eat and drink before the storm hit."

"Then Elijah went to pray."

"Then he went to pray. Climbed to the top of the mountain and put his face between his knees."

Sarah turned the forage cap over in her hands. "Why would he do that?"

"It was an important prayer before the Lord God Almighty. Nowadays people think they can just sit with God at the cracker barrel and talk with him as if they are his equal. No one is his equal. Do you understand that?"

"Yes."

"Seven times Elijah told his servant to go and look towards the sea. Even though the servant saw nothing Elijah was expecting an answer to his prayer. It didn't come right away but he continued to believe and he continued to pray on his knees. He persisted."

"I know. If you are convinced something is right and that it's from God you keep pursuing it no matter what."

He kissed the top of her head. "You are one of my best cadets."

"Will I ever get a uniform?"

"We'll see." He picked up a few smooth stones and tossed them in his palm. "The seventh time the servant saw a cloud no bigger than this." Uncle Thomas closed his fist over the stones. "It was rising from the ocean."

"Harness your horse! Get in your chariot! If you don't go down the mountain quickly the storm will sweep away the road!"

Uncle Thomas nodded. "That's what Elijah told the servant to say to the king. And even though the king had done evil things he still believed in God and he still believed Elijah was God's prophet. So he hitched his horses to his chariot and down the mountain he and his driver flew. The sky went black. The small fist of cloud that came from prayer was now so big it covered the heavens. And wind. A great, great wind made clouds of dust swirl on the earth. The power of the Lord God of Hosts seized Elijah and he began to run. Tucked the ends of his robe into his belt so his legs were free and raced ahead of King Ahab down the mountain road and into Jezreel."

"He ran faster than the horses!" Sarah almost shouted.

"He did. That was the Lord God Almighty working in him. You can do the improbable and what men consider the impossible if you work hand in glove with the Lord of Hosts. Yet it all began with raindrops. Small raindrops. No more than that."

Sarah smiled for this was her favorite part of her uncle's storytelling. "Elijah on his knees. Praying seven times in a row. His servant going to look seven times in a row. A cloud no bigger than a man's fist."

He smiled back at her. "Little spatters of rain in the dust. Dust that hadn't seen water in three and a half years. Tiny drops, my girl. But it presaged a downpour that refreshed and renewed the entire land and bathed her in righteousness."

She planted the forage cap back on his head. "I've been thinking about this, uncle. Your life started with raindrops too. First you were a boy. Then a young man. After that a soldier who fought in Mexico. Now the raindrops are getting bigger and bigger and you are a teacher at a famous school. Who knows when your downpour will come?"

"My downpour, eh?" Uncle Thomas got to his feet and brushed dirt and twigs off his blue uniform pants. "We'd best get back to the house or your mom'll skin me alive. It's getting on to dinnertime."

Sarah took his hand and walked beside him through the trees. "What about my raindrops?"

"Why, it's the same as it was for me. The Lord takes you from a baby to the girl you are now. Small pinpricks of rain. But one day you will finish school, turn eighteen, be a young woman, fall in love, marry, have children of your own. Then you'll have your own downpour."

"What will my downpour be? I'm not going to be a professor or an officer in the army and do brave deeds."

"How do you know you won't do brave deeds? It's not only soldiers in the army who act with courage or fight battles. Elijah wasn't a soldier in the army of Israel but he was certainly a soldier in the army of God and look at what a difference his bravery made. Only the Lord knows what your downpour will be like, my girl. One day you could be mistress of your own plantation and think of what a great thing that would be and all the good you could do. Pray and remain faithful and watch the raindrops fall. Some day you will hear the sound of heavy rain here." He tapped his head with his finger. "Or here." He patted his heart. "Then you will know your moment has arrived. God Almighty will pour his righteousness down on you. And many will be blessed. Not just yourself. It is never just for yourself. Many will be blessed."

She hugged her arm to him. "Uncle, you sound so sure of what God is going to do for me and you. You sound so sure of yourself."

"Well, Sarah, I suppose I am sure of myself because I am sure of the God I serve. Come, what have you memorized this past month? What Bible verses can you recite to me?"

"I have memorized a whole two chapters in the Gospel of John, uncle."

He laughed, glancing down and admiring her. "Have you? Let us hear them as we walk."

"All right. *In the beginning was the Word and the Word was with God and the Word was God.*"

"Amen. The best beginning of all. Carry on, my girl, carry on, we are still a good ways from the house."

1853

"Sarah!"

She knew her uncle would search for her among the seven old oak trees that gave the plantation its name so she was several hundred feet behind them in a thick bush.

"Sarah! We are back from our honeymoon and I want to see you!" Her uncle was not in his uniform but wore a shirt, tie, brown waistcoat and pants and sported a broad-brimmed hat. "Why, Ellie wants to see you as well!"

Sarah remained hidden, watching her uncle go from oak tree to oak tree.

"Come, Sarah, you told me you enjoyed the wedding. And Ellie thinks you're sweet. I've told her how mature you are for a ten year old. Don't disappoint me." He glanced around, dark lines beginning to form at his eyes. "This is nonsense. You knew I would get married one day and that I would not be able to marry you. Aren't you my Christian warrior? Show me your mettle." He removed his hat and sat on a moss-covered stump. "We had intended to bring you home with us for a week. Your mother and father have given their approval. I told you Ellie's father was president of Washington College, didn't I? They have put an addition on his home for Ellie and I. There is a special bedroom for you. That is where we should like you to sleep. A special doll is waiting for you who has an elegant hooped dress."

Sarah darted out from the bush. "Oh, what color is the dress?"

Anger and relief passed over her uncle's face like swiftly moving clouds.

"What should I have done about this sort of behavior if you were one of my cadets?" Uncle Thomas growled.

"I'm not a cadet. I don't have the uniform you promised me."

"Is that so?"

She put her hand in his. "I only need to pack. What color is her dress?"

Uncle Thomas pushed himself to his feet, still scowling but still holding his niece's hand. "Whose dress?"

"The doll's, of course."

"Why, it's red."

"Red. Scarlet. Crimson. Vermillion. *Rouge. Rubrum. Roseus. Rojo.*"

He half-smiled and grumbled, "At least your languages are coming along. That's something."

"Red is my favorite color, uncle," she said as they walked through the woods to the house.

"I knew that," he replied.

1854

"Miss Sarah!"

Billy King stood with his hands on his hips by the oak trees.

"Now, this ain't a time for more of your tricks. And if you've messed up your mourning outfit your mama will have a fit."

Crouched behind a boulder nicked orange with lichen, Sarah put a hand over her eyes as the tears came again, burning quick paths across her face.

"Come along, Miss Sarah. If there was ever a time your uncle needed you it's today. Burying his child and his wife. No man so young should have to do that. Come along now. As God is my witness it'll break his heart all over again if you don't attend the funeral."

"It's not right!" Sarah cried out from behind the boulder. "It isn't fair! Why would God do that to him?"

"God didn't do nothing to him, Miss Sarah. It's life and the devil stillborn his son and brought on the bleeding that took Mrs. Jackson."

"Why didn't God stop it?"

"This world is a mix of good and evil, Miss Sarah; you know that. It's not heaven. What God's doing now is healing your uncle. But he needs your help."

"He doesn't need my help if he's God."

"Probably not," grunted Billy. "But he set it up that way. It's his rules. He decided he'd work through people like me and you and that's what he does. It ain't for you to argue with him."

"Ellie was so sweet to me!"

"I know it."

"I wrapped the doll with the red dress that she gave me in black."

"I seen where you put her on the chair in the parlor."

"If I could move the doll's hands I'd put them over her face."

"I expect you would."

"I don't want to see the coffins." She could barely speak as her throat tightened. "I don't want to see the graves."

"No one does. Especially a lady like yourself. But there's things we have got to do. And a lady standing tall and straight at a family funeral is one of them. They all need you today, Miss Sarah. Your Uncle Thomas needs you most of all. Won't you come? The carriage is waiting."

She stood up from behind the boulder, her eyes red, her black silk dress wrinkled. Billy rushed to her side and wiped her face with the black lace handkerchief she clutched in one hand.

"There now," he soothed. "There now. Straighten your dress some. Smooth it down with your hands. That's taken most of the wrinkles out. Smooth it down again. Your face is looking as sad as I've ever seen it. Your eyes are red as blood and swollen up. That's what the veil is for. Where's your hat?"

"Right by my feet."

"Let's put it on." He placed the black hat on her head and adjusted it. "Your pins are still holding your hair up well enough. Drop the veil now."

The black lace veil covered her face.

"You can't see the red and puffiness anymore. That's fine. Where's your gloves? Put them on."

She pulled on the black lace gloves.

"Here's your hanky back." He studied her. "It's a pity it's such a mourning day because you do look every inch a lady of Virginia. You're tall for your age and straight as a hickory rod. But there'll be other days when you can shine. Today you just need to be as strong and true as one of these oaks. All right now. Can we get to that carriage?"

"Yes, Billy."

They walked side by side through the undergrowth, Sarah lifting the hem of her dress as they went. After five minutes they came in sight of the dark brown brick walls of the house and the stately white columns that always seemed to her to reach to the clouds. Two black horses and a black carriage stood in the drive. Her parents and three brothers were talking quietly beside it. All heads turned as Sarah emerged from the forest. She stood as tall as she had ever stood.

"Thank you, Billy," she said as he slipped away to the back of the house.

He turned and smiled back at her. "It is always an honor to serve you, Miss Sarah."

1857

Sarah, in a scarlet dress with a four hoop skirt underneath, walked hand in hand with Uncle Thomas, wearing his blue uniform, along a new flagstone pathway that led to the back of the mansion and down into the woods.

"Billy laid this last year," she said.

"He did a good job."

"It actually goes all the way to the seven oaks."

"Is that because Billy grew tired of having to fight his way through the brush every time he needed to find you?"

Sarah laughed. "Well, I've put away childish things now. Thank you for this birthday present." Still holding his hand, she dropped back a few steps and curtsied. "Why, I'd be honored to have this dance with you, sir."

He inclined his head. "The dress suits you. Please wear it to the wedding ball."

"I intend to. I hope there will be some dashing cadets there."

"A few, I suppose. But you will be chaperoned, my dear, by the heaviest artillery I can muster. You imagine yourself all of eighteen or nineteen or twenty." He wagged a thick finger. "I have it on the best authority you are fourteen. Still a child."

Her face took on the hue of her dress. "I am not a child."

"You are – "

"A young woman. At least entitle me to be a young woman in your eyes if I am not yet allowed to be a lady."

"Very well." He smiled into his brown beard. "You comport yourself like a lady, it's true. You speak like one and your manners are elegant. You are certainly one of the most gracious daughters of one of the most gracious families in Virginia. But fourteen. Only fourteen."

"I can't help that, Uncle Thomas."

They continued to walk together, her hand still in his.

"Do you like Mary Anna?" he asked.

"Your fiancée is a lady of great charm and warmth. I adore her. Will I be able to visit the two of you after your marriage?"

"Naturally. There is always the spare bedroom for my niece."

As they walked Uncle Thomas held his free hand up over his head. Sarah scarcely noticed. She knew he did this because he felt one arm was shorter than the other and that raising his arm improved the circulation in his body. After a few minutes of quiet Sarah decided to ask him what was uppermost in her mind.

"Uncle, you have just come through a season of dryness."

"Mm."

"Where were your raindrops from God?"

He did not answer for a moment but pointed to a bench that had been placed by the seven oaks. "We will sit there. Are you able to do that in your dress?"

"It's only four hoops, Uncle. I'll be alright."

The sun made its way through the oak leaves overhead so that a pattern of shade and light moved back and forth over her uncle's face and beard. She waited for him to answer her question. He did not look at her but stared straight ahead.

"My childhood was difficult," he began. "There is no need for me to go into all the details. Father died of typhoid when I was two. Mother remarried when I was six. My father had been an attorney and so was this man. But he did not like me or my sister and brother. The three of us were sent away. I lived in various homes, some decent, some cruel. It was a dry season. Yet even through those years there were the raindrops of God Almighty's mercies – my uncle Cummins Jackson was a fair man to me, hard, but fair."

He took a lemon from the pocket of his frock coat, polished it on the sleeve of his uniform and bit into it, chewing the rind and pulp and all. "West Point was another dry season at first. I was eighteen. With all my living with different relatives my book learning had suffered. But I found I liked the discipline of the military life and realized the Lord had brought me to where I was meant to be. So I put my head down and applied myself. West Point was a rainfall for me. Fighting in the Mexican War confirmed my sense that God was calling me to be a soldier."

He stopped to chew and swallow. Then he pulled two oranges out of another pocket and offered her one. She thanked him and held it in her lap while he began to peel his with a small pocketknife, popping segments into his mouth. When he finished he wiped the blade on the grass by his left boot.

"You know the rest," he said. "Losing my wife and child was a double saber blow. I fought back with prayer and faith. They are in a better place; I believe that, although I miss them very much. So my hope in the Lord is the rain for my parched soul. My trip to Europe last year was a refreshing shower as well. I do not like to speak of it but you have proven to be a tight-lipped confidante so I will say not all my students approve of me. They do not cotton to my religious zeal or the discipline I seek to instill in them which permits them to succeed. While I was on the other side of the ocean a number of alumni attempted to have me removed from my position." He raised his arm as if he was calling on God to be his witness but Sarah knew it was for the improvement of his circulation. "They did not succeed. In such testings of life, dear girl, it is indeed like a dry and burning desert. You may not see the rainfall you need to green the heart, not for months or years. But there will always be raindrops. And one day the showers that bless. So you put your head down and carry on with what you believe is right. God will send the smattering of drops your way that remind you he is watching over you and your ways." His arm remained in the air.

"Mary Anna is more than a smattering of raindrops, I should think," Sarah teased.

"Indeed. A sun shower, my girl."

"Complete with a rainbow."

A small smile passed over his lips. "It's nice to think of it that way."

1858

May 26th
My dearest Uncle Thomas

    I have prayed for you and Mary Anna without ceasing once our household received the terrible news. I cannot think of what to say except what you have told me so many times: There is a merciful God, there is a beautiful Heaven, and your daughter is with him who loves her more than you or I ever could, even though my love for your baby is great, and your father's love for her even greater.
    I think of how I held her when she was but a week old and my tears fall like rain. That she did not live to see a month of days seems a harsh thing to me. I know you will tell me God has ordained what he has ordained and it is our duty to accept his decrees. Yet I recall our Lord wept at his friend's grave and that he wept over Jerusalem as well. Indeed he felt great compassion for the widow of Nain who had lost her only son. If all this be so then I feel free to weep as Jesus wept, and I feel free to have compassion on you and your wife for you have lost your only daughter. I accept God's ways, for he is our Lord and Master, and I commit your sweet baby to his eternal care. I know she has abundant life in a way we can never enjoy this side of Heaven. At the same time I weep with those who weep and I bear in mind Solomon's wise words: There is a time to weep, there is a time to mourn. So I grieve with you and Mary Anna, as a good Christian ought, and I also look to our heavenly Father who holds your infant daughter in his bosom where she is safe and cherished.
    The Lord bless you and Mary Anna in this hard season. The Lord bless your daughter Mary Graham in Paradise.
    We leave tomorrow, Thursday the 27th, for Lexington to be at your side and to stand with you at the funeral. There will be a full moon. It will shine on us, uncle, and remind us of the love of God.
    My prayers and deepest affection
    Your niece
    Sarah Felicity Nunley

1859

My dear Sarah

I wish to announce I have purchased a house in Lexington. I thought it best to remove Mary Anna and myself to a new location and begin afresh. The address is 8 East Washington Street. It was built in 1801 and is a solid structure, all brick to the front and all stone to the back. There is a large balcony as well and enough space in the yard for a vegetable garden. The house itself is roomy and both Mary Anna and myself like the way it is laid out very much.

I have written your parents in expectation of a visit. All three of your brothers are cadets at the Virginia Military Institute so it would make a great deal of sense to combine a visit to us with a visit to them. And you are sixteen! There is an autumn ball you shall want to attend. I will permit you to have an escort, one of your brothers preferably, and to enjoy the company of our young Southern gentleman. I will, naturally, as your uncle and in my position as a professor at the Institute, take the first dance, if I may. I have no doubt at all in my mind that you will be the belle of the ball.

In addition, my wife and I should like to extend an invitation for you to stay with us a week or longer. Mary Anna always enjoys your company and you would bring welcome laughter, youthfulness, and a young woman's charm to our four walls. I will, of course, mention this invitation to your mother and father as well, with the hope that they will see clear to granting you leave to remain with us. A two week stay, though perhaps too much to hope for, would be a splendid housewarming gift for us.

Finally, I will say that upon your arrival at our home for your visit you will find, I think, a most happy set of clothing laid out upon your bed. Do you dare to guess what it will be? While you may not wear it to the ball – we shall ensure our sixteen year old has something gracious and ladylike and practical to wear to that – other occasions shall certainly afford themselves where you might don the attire and mingle in public along with Mary Anna and myself. So that is something else for you to look forward to along with setting foot in our new home, having a splendid bedroom of your own, and waltzing at the Institute's autumn ball. I trust all the above will be sufficient to entice you from the woods and portals of Seven Oaks, lovely as that plantation may be.

Mary Anna and I look forward to your response in high hopes we will not be disappointed.

God bless you and direct your steps in even so small an affair as this.

Yours most truly
Uncle Thomas
Major T.J. Jackson
Professor of Natural and Experimental Philosophy
Instructor of Artillery
Virginia Military Institute
Lexington, Rockingham County
Commonwealth of Virginia

"And thine ears shall hear a word behind thee, saying, This is the way, walk ye in it, when ye turn to the right hand, and when ye turn to the left." The thirtieth chapter of Isaiah and verse twenty-one

1860

"Shall I step down and adjust your stirrups for you, uncle?"

"I'm perfectly fine."

"But they are set too short. Your legs are almost bent double. It must hurt your knees."

"Not at all. It gives me a better sense of control."

"Suit yourself."

Sarah rode alongside Uncle Thomas as they made their way down a curving dirt track near the plantation's tobacco fields. She wore the blue uniform with brass buttons he had given her the year before. It was an exact replica of the uniform he wore at the Virginia Military Institute and which he was wearing as he walked his mount beside hers. The sun was hot and they both had the blue forage cap on their heads.

"It is hard work." Sarah reined in and watched the slaves picking the tobacco. "And very hot for this time of year."

"It is," her uncle replied.

"You have six slaves now, don't you?"

"Yes."

"Are they happy with their situation?"

He shrugged. "Amy cooks and cleans and does very well at it. Albert wants to work out his freedom so I have arranged for him to be employed at a hotel in Lexington. In addition I rent him out to the

Institute and he does some labor there. Hetty and her two sons Cyrus and George I keep busy – you should see my vegetable garden that they tend. And sweet little four year old Emma, well, she is five or six now – "

Sarah laughed. "I adored playing dolls with her."

He nodded. "She responded to you admirably. You helped her with her learning handicap in the same gentle manner Mary Anna does."

"You never told me how you came by Emma."

"A gift from a very old widow." He followed the movements of two strong young men as they bent over a stack of tobacco leaves. "Slavery is what it is. I expect it will not last forever. For now the Holy Bible admonishes us to treat them fairly and with dignity. You do that at Seven Oaks, thanks be to God."

She gazed at a family working together. "Paul says that if a slave can win his freedom he should do it."

"Yes."

"And he sent Onesimus back to his master a true Christian. Paul wanted the master to treat him like a Christian brother."

"Mm. Paul was right to expect that. Though the slave would not have been African."

"Mama tells me you do a great deal for the African people in Lexington. Slaves and free men."

He grunted. "It is only right. It is what God would have us do. To help them better their situation. And to know the love and mercy of our Lord. They must not be left in ignorance of that great truth. Indeed they should not be left in ignorance of anything good. They thrive in the Sunday School class at our Presbyterian church."

"I am so glad to hear that." She fixed her brown eyes on his face. "If I were ever mistress of Seven Oaks I should set my slaves free, uncle. If they wished to remain with us I would let them but I would pay them fair wages."

The blue in his eyes deepened. "Your words don't shock me, my dear. You have always been one to know how to keep your lips sealed so I shall tell you a secret. Much of my learning before West Point had to be self-taught. Now and then I saw the inside of a classroom but I knew if I truly wished to improve I should have to do it for myself. I struck a deal with a slave on my Uncle Cummins' farm – he would provide me with pine knots and I would teach him how to read books and how to write. No one knew about this. We both would have been whipped. Or worse. Virginia law is dead against giving instruction in writing and reading to slaves or free men or even mulattos."

"I know."

"But I did it anyways because I felt God Almighty telling me it was right." He smiled. "And because I needed those pine knots. I used them at night after the day's work was done. I read by their light. That's how I learned enough to get off to a half-decent start at West Point."

Sarah's eyes shone gold at the thought of him turning pages while others slept. "Weren't you tired in the mornings?"

"I taught myself not to be tired."

"That sounds like you. What happened to the slave?"

"Once I'd given him all the learning I could, he lit out for the British territories by means of the underground railroad – Canada. The other slaves gave me to understand he made it. I was pleased when I heard that." He tugged a lemon out of his pocket and bit into it. "The boy was young and strong and blessed by the Lord with an uncommon mind and zeal. He deserved a chance at a life."

Sarah began to walk her horse again and Uncle Thomas took his place on her right.

"Will we secede, uncle?" she asked.

He chewed on his lemon a few moments before replying. "Virginia is not as keen on it as South Carolina and Mississippi."

"What if Abraham Lincoln should be elected president?"

"Why, he is perceived as an abolitionist. Certainly that will scare some folk off. But secession is a serious matter. Virginia would not jump in with both feet. I took an oath to defend the United States of America. Every soldier in Virginia did."

"Is it just the fear that slavery will be tampered with by Mr. Lincoln?"

"No. Some resent Washington for wanting more and more of our wealth. A bigger slice of the cash pie from our crops, especially the profits from cotton. There are many reasons."

"I do not want to see secession, uncle."

"Nor do I. I pray to Almighty God for cooler heads to prevail. But if Virginia should withdraw from the union I know where I must stand, my dear. Before loyalty to a nation a man stands by his family and his home. In the eyes of God, home and hearth come before capitals and politics and government decrees. I would unsheathe my sword for the Commonwealth."

She bit her lower lip. "I do not like to hear you speak this way. I read a book on the civil war in England. Oliver Cromwell and the Roundheads against the Royalists. It was terrible."

"Sometimes I react too aggressively. Secession does not mean civil war will follow. Washington may well let us go our way in peace."

"And split the nation the British could not split a hundred years ago?"

He brought an apple from his frock coat and began to eat it, not offering any response.

"What does God want?" she prodded him.

He spoke between swallows. "I do not know. We have not even had the presidential election. Who knows what the South will truly do this fall and winter? Nothing at all may come to pass. This year may roll on into the next without any incidents whatsoever."

The lines on her face came together in a sharp frown. "How could it be easy for you to unsheathe your sword, as you said? How could it be easy for you to take up arms against the land you swore before God to defend?"

He took the apple from his mouth. His blues flashed. "I did not say it would be easy."

"But – "

"I am a soldier. I know what war costs. Drilling is preferable to killing. Yet I also know this – *If the thing is to be done let it be done quickly.* Fast movement, hard strikes, the pursuit of a routed foe, bringing all manner of weaponry to bear including artillery, everything must be employed in order to win swiftly and completely. As gruesome as it may seem, such actions end a war rather than prolong it. Therefore they save more lives rather than bleed many thousands away as slow-witted generals always do, blast them, waging their interminable conflicts."

"You sound too eager."

"Do I? I suppose I am not afraid of war in the sense that many are afraid of it because I am not afraid of death. My time to depart is fixed in heaven. So when I fight, I fight, and boldly go where others would not. Such aggression ends battles quickly and decisively. I will not die before the Lord has decreed I ought to die so I have no fear and do what must be done to bring about a victory. That is how I learned to think in Mexico ten years ago."

She stopped her horse under the shade of a young oak tree. He studied her face, threw the apple core from him, brought his mount closer, and laid his gloved hand on her arm.

"It was not my intention to trouble your spirit. I have a military ardor and it rises up in me like fire once the trumpet blows. But the truth is I would rather enjoy hearth and home than be out on battlefields defending them. Let me have my wife by my side, yes, and my niece, and a house full of children, and peas and beans to pick in my back yard – that is how I should like to spend my time. Make no mistake, if I must fight, I'll strike like a lightning bolt and let go with all my cannon. But only so I can have what I crave most – my home unmolested, my family at peace, my liberty secure." He squeezed her arm and drew his hand back. "Believe me, I'd rather have a bowl of peaches or a plate of watermelon than a kettle full of army food no matter how well stirred."

She laughed. "You and your peaches and lemons and watermelon. I believe you mean it when you say that."

"I do mean it."

"I shall pray against war."

"Do that, my girl. But bear in mind that often enough God gives men their head and lets their actions and their folly play out completely. What is going to happen in 1861 is already established in the heavens."

"But what if I feel led to pray?"

"Why, then, you must pray, my dear, for the Holy Ghost is prompting you. Your prayers are part of his plan. They may stop secession or stop a war."

She knew the fear and sadness she felt had taken over her eyes and mouth and face. "What if there is a war?"

Her uncle moved his horse back in the direction of the mansion, squinting as he came out into full sunlight again. "Then your prayers will direct its course and its duration. Who knows the mind of God? Who can tell him what is or is not best? Pray your prayers and accept God's will." He turned his head with its forage cap and smiled back at her. "And don't forget to pray for your old uncle. Pray they don't put me out to pasture whatever happens. I'm almost forty. Suppose they decide I'm not young enough to wage war or wage peace? Suppose they decide it's best I stir that kettle full of bad meat and rotten potatoes? I don't think I could stand it. I might do something rash."

She rode slowly after him. "When do you do anything rash, sir?"

He did not answer for a moment and then asked, "Have you kept up with your Scripture memorization?"

"I have."

"Where are you with that, my dear?"

"Psalms. I have been practicing Psalm 144 this week."

"Ah. *Blessed be the Lord my strength which teacheth my hands to war and my fingers to fight.*"

"Yes, sir."

"Finish it for me as we ride. The words are greatness itself."

"Pray take care, uncle." She had come alongside him. "In politics one thing leads to another and rarely to a good end."

He glanced at her. "I shall be wary if it should come to blows."

"I pray for you and Mary Anna every day."

"It is well you do so, Sarah. Thank you."

"I want you to give me away at my wedding."

His blue eyes opened up. "Give you away? Wedding? I have heard nothing of this. Who is the beau? Why will your father not give you away?"

She smiled. "I have no beau. But when the day comes I wish for you to be the one who releases me to him. I have mentioned this to father and he does not object."

Uncle Thomas laughed. "What a strange gal you are. Planning everything out as if you had a map and a regiment."

"Yes. And a compass. Not so strange. I picked up the habit from you."

He laughed again, a deep rumbling in his chest and throat that fought its way through his mouth and beard. "Why, then, I should be honored. The Lord's name be praised."

Sarah looked ahead to the dark tunnel of oak branches and deep green leaves they were about to pass through. "The Lord's name be praised now and forevermore."

She began to recite the rest of the psalm as they entered the shadows.

My goodness and my fortress. My high tower and my deliverer. My shield and he in whom I trust, who subdueth my people under me.

Lord, what is man, that thou takest knowledge of him! Or the son of man, that thou makest account of him!

Man is like to vanity, his days are as a shadow that passeth away.

Bow thy heavens, oh Lord, and come down. Touch the mountains and they shall smoke.

Cast forth lightning and scatter them. Shoot out thine arrows and destroy them.

Send thine hand from above. Rid me and deliver me out of great waters, from the hand of strange children

Whose mouth speaketh vanity and their right hand is a right hand of falsehood.

I will sing a new song unto thee, oh God. Upon a psaltery and an instrument of ten strings will I sing praises unto thee.

It is he that giveth salvation unto kings, who delivereth David his servant from the hurtful sword.

Rid me and deliver me from the hand of strange children, whose mouth speaketh vanity and their right hand is a right hand of falsehood.

That our sons may be as plants grown up in their youth, that our daughters may be as corner stones, polished after the similitude of a palace,

That our garners may be full, affording all manner of store, that our sheep may bring forth thousands and ten thousands in our streets,

That our oxen may be strong to labor, that there be no breaking in, nor going out, that there be no complaining in our streets.

Happy is that people, that is in such a case, yea, happy is that people, whose God is the Lord.

"Amen," rumbled Uncle Thomas. "I like that very well, my girl. You speak the sacred words beautifully." He relaxed his grip on the reins in his gloved hands. "I shall take it as a sign from the Lord, this psalm coming after our talk of the possibility of perilous river crossings ahead of us. I will take it to heart as my Scripture for 1861 and the years after it, come what may." He twisted in his saddle and placed his bright blue eyes on her. "Do you approve?"

"There is a great deal of good in the verses." She hesitated. "And in you, uncle."

"In me?" He shook his head. "None is good but God." He urged his horse forward. "I have had my falls from grace."

"*A just man falls seven times and rises up again.*"

"By the mercy of God."

"Yes, sir," she responded. They emerged into the sunlight once again and she drew up on his right shoulder. "By the mercy of God."

Stonewall

1861

Dear Sarah

I thought up until the end the conflict could be avoided, but now what's done is done and we must fight. The Old Dominion has seceded and you and I are citizens of a new country. I am being sent to Richmond with my cadets and that, of course, includes your three brothers.

But war or no war you are eighteen and a ball is being held in your honor at Seven Oaks. We are fighting for hearth and home and that means our precious families and women folk. I am making arrangements for the cadets and myself to come by the plantation on our way to the capital. It is out of our way but no matter. My boys will comport themselves in a manner worthy of Virginia and our new nation, I can assure you, and will bring a good deal of gaiety to your coming of age celebration. I am sending a gown on ahead of the event that Mary Ann has picked out and that I hope you will wear. Naturally I reserve the right to first dance after your father and would be happy to pronounce a prayer of God's blessing over the occasion.

I trust I will see you in a few days.
With love and affection,
Uncle Thomas

"Is he here?"

"Yes, Miss Sarah, they are all here – your uncle, your brothers, and the cadets Major Jackson brought with him from Lexington."

Sarah poked her head out of the door of her room. "May I tiptoe to the head of the staircase and take a peek?"

"Well, I – " began the female slave.

"No, Miss Sarah, y'all may not." Another female slave in her room was fussing with Sarah's hair. "We all need at least another ten minutes."

"All rights, Harriet," said the woman in the hallway, "but Major Jackson is champing at the bit to say his prayer, have his dance, and get his young soldiers to Richmond."

"Well, let him champ away. A lady is only eighteen once and there's but the one coming of age party for her."

"Mm-hm. I'll tell them ten minutes. But the young women the Nunleys invited to the ball are just as champing as the major and his cadets."

"Are they?" Harriet smiled as she positioned Sarah's ringlets on her shoulders. "What about her brothers? What about Warren and Christopher and Samuel? How do they look?"

"I haven't seen them in ages and now they don't look like boys no more. They're grown men."

Sarah's eyes filled with light. "Each of them looks dashing?"

"Yes, Miss."

"Each of them is in his gray cadet uniform?"

"Yes, Miss."

"Do any of their classmates look quite so handsome, Letta?"

Letta smiled. "None. But there are some mighty close seconds. If I was you, Miss Sarah, after you dances with your father and uncle and brothers, why, I'd stick like a tic to Major Jackson. There's a couple of the young men glued to his right and left shoulders like gold braid who are at his beck and call. Either of them would do well for a lady's slow waltz."

"Thank you, Letta. I shall heed your advice."

After another fifteen minutes had gone by Sarah was ready to descend the staircase. She wore a silk burgundy gown over wide hoop skirts that held six bones and a ruby pendant glittered at her throat. Her father, who she spotted standing next to Uncle Thomas at the bottom of the stairs, had wrapped the bannister in deep crimson bunting and hung Confederate flags of seven stars and three broad red and white stripes in the front entryway. He was in the finely tailored gray uniform of a Confederate captain while her uncle wore the blue frock coat and pants he always used to lecture in at the Virginia Military Institute. The young men in cadet gray who stood at Uncle Thomas' shoulders were indeed tall and handsome and their eyes followed her descent so closely and eagerly she felt a warm blush creep up from her neck to her cheeks.

"My dear." Her father extended his bent arm. "You are the eighth star in the Confederate flag."

"Hear, hear," said her uncle. "Does the gown please you, Sarah?"

"Very much, Uncle Thomas. Please thank your wife the next time you see her for her impeccable taste."

"Alas, it will be some time before I lay eyes on *mi bella esposa*. But I shall certainly write her from Richmond and extend your compliments." He tapped her father on the arm. "Remember that I have the second dance, Grayson, and that I outrank you."

Her father smiled. "Who could forget with you glowering by the punch bowl and waiting your turn with all the patience of a cavalry charge?"

"May I have the third, Miss?" blurted one of her uncle's young aides, stepping forward. "It would make my night, why, it would make my year, and I am going off to war for you."

"You are?" responded Sarah in surprise.

The other young man also stepped forward and bowed. "Will Carpenter, Miss. Please honor me with the fourth dance. I am also going to war for you."

"Steady in the harness," rumbled her uncle. "Don't pitch the cannon in the ditch before it's had a chance to fire."

The young men shrank back but Sarah saw the humor pass swiftly in and out of her uncle's eyes and smiled at the two cadets.

"Why, I would love that," she replied. "How on earth could I refuse a dance to either of the two gentlemen who are ready to die for me? Please approach me after I have waltzed with my father and uncle."

"Yes, Miss."

"Thank you, Miss."

She came into the ballroom on her father's arm and hundreds of guests, men in suits and uniforms, women in gowns, cadets in gray, began to applaud. The room was draped in more Confederate flags and more crimson bunting. Candles and oil lamps burned from one end of the room to the other. A small band stood ready to play on her father's signal. Her mother came up to them just before he raised his hand to the bandleader.

"My dear, you are absolutely ravishing." Her mother was thin and light but her large smile made her seem twice her size and height. "Letta and Harriet certainly worked wonders with your hair. You look like a princess out of a story book."

"Thank you, mama. How are you feeling?"

"Oh, crowds and heat are never my strong suit. If I feel faint I shall step out onto the front porch and take the evening air."

"How is your heart? The doctor said – "

"Oh, my heart is beating away just like everyone else's here. Never mind me. Just enjoy yourself. You are a lady today."

Her father lifted his arm, the band began to play a waltz, and he swept around the spacious ballroom with Sarah while people applauded a second time. No sooner had he finished than her uncle took her in his arms and moved her carefully and sturdily over the floor. Then the band struck up a Virginia reel and before either of the two cadets could present themselves her brothers had spirited her away to one of several groups where men and women faced one another in two long lines. She was whirled and twirled and her ringlets spun in the air and she laughed so hard she could not get her breath.

"What are you doing, Warren?" she gasped as he danced furiously down between the lines of men and women with her.

He grinned. "Why, keeping you safe from the Virginia Military Institute, of course."

"But I want to dance with those young men."

"No, you don't."

"Yes, I do."

"Leave Will Carpenter and his buddy Sid Thornbush to the punch bowl and the other young women. Chris and Sam and I have someone special in mind for you."

"You mean besides yourselves?"

He laughed and his impish grin made Sarah laugh too.

They both got back in line and began to clap the rhythm while another couple swung down the corridor between the men and women. One reel was followed by another reel until perspiration formed along Sarah's hairline and just above her lip. Drawing a fan out of a pocket in her gown she waved it back and forth over her face as the cadets finally made their way to her lineup and took turns reeling her up and down the line.

"Where is this hero you've picked out for me?" Sarah asked her brother Christopher as he spun her in a circle soon after Will Carpenter had just done the same.

"I don't know, Felicity." He always used her middle name, claiming the name Sarah was too common.

"Didn't you all come together?"

"Sure, but his parents are only a mile away so father let him borrow a horse from our stables and pay them a quick visit."

"What?" Sarah dragged him out of the line to a wall covered by a huge Confederate flag. "A mile away? I must know him and his family, Christopher Nunley."

"No one said you didn't know him."

"Warren made it sound like it was some big surprise."

"Well, it will be."

"Oh, yes, I'm sure it will be. Who is it? Billy Stringer? Tom Washington? No, don't tell me, it's Malcolm the Mouse."

Her brother said nothing.

Her eyes flared. "You can't be serious. It's Malcolm?"

"Yes, but – "

She swatted him on the arm. "For heaven's sakes! You three brats had my hopes up! I thought I was going to meet Sir Galahad! Malcolm Becket Ross! Pardon me while I go drown myself in the punch bowl!"

"It's not what you think."

"Not what I think? What do y'all think I think?"

"That he's puny and scrawny with bad hair and bad skin."

Sarah put her hands on her hips as the band continued to play reels and the cadets and young women danced all around them.

"Isn't he? Or are you saying there has been a great miracle since he turned fifteen four years ago? Because that's the last time I saw him and a hound dog full of tics looked better than he did that day."

Christopher shrugged. "Okay, there's been a miracle."

"Oh, there has? A biblical *he turned the water into wine* kind of miracle?"

"I guess."

"You guess?" She swatted his arm again. "We don't see miracles like that anymore, little brother. The day of miracles is over, the preachers tell us. No parting of the Red Sea. No healing of the lepers. No raising of the dead."

Chris jerked his chin toward the ballroom doors. "There's the corpse."

Sarah glared at her brother and glared at the doors. A tall young man, his gray uniform spotted by raindrops, had just entered, cap under his arm, and appeared to be searching for his friends amidst the swirl of dancers. His hair was black as night and perfectly combed, his eyes blue as a morning sky, his skin as clean and tight as well-washed linen, his shoulders broad, and when he smiled at something Major Jackson said to him, the smile was sunlight on a river.

"What?" Sarah stared at him and then stared at her brother. "That's not him. You're not going to tell me that's him."

"It is him."

"It is not."

"Shall I wave him over and introduce the two of you to each other?"

"Don't you dare. My face is still red from all those Virginia reels."

Chris raised his arm. After a moment the newcomer noticed it, grinned, and started to make his way across the dance floor to them.

"Still a brat." Sarah hit her brother a third time.

"Some things don't change. Even if Malcolm Becket Ross does. Of course I could introduce him as Sir Galahad if that would make you feel better."

"If you do that – "

But Sarah could not complete her threat for the tall dark-haired cadet was upon them. He shook Christopher's hand and then bowed to Sarah.

"Sarah Nunley," he said, "I was just outside admiring a night full of stars. It was not half so beautiful as you."

Sarah was so surprised by his first sentence she did not respond.

"I have not seen you in, what, four years? And here you are, a lady, and outshining anyone I see here, young or old."

Sarah finally found her tongue as her brother watched, a large smile cracking open his freckled face.

"Good evening, sir, I am not used to getting bombarded with gallantries from a Virginia Military Institute cadet."

"Or from Malcolm the Mouse either."

She could feel a flush darting over her face. "As you say, it has been a number of years. We hardly know each other anymore."

"Well, let's change that, shall we?" He bowed again. "They have given up the reel for the waltz. May I have this dance, Sarah Nunley?"

Awkwardly, she gave him her hand. "All right."

His arm was firm across her back, his steps sure, his smile warm. They glided across the dance floor as if there were no other couples they needed to be aware of. She saw her three brothers standing together joining Christopher in his grin, glimpsed her father dancing with her mother, spotted Uncle Thomas watching her swoop past in Malcolm's arms without a shred of emotion on his face. The scent of his hair and the spice of the cologne on Malcolm's skin were so pleasant she closed her eyes and almost leaned her head on his shoulder.

What do I do now that the mouse has become a lion? And the most handsome lion in the forest at that?

"This must be so exciting for you," said Malcolm.

At first she thought he meant she was excited he was dancing with her and was about to retort when she saw by his eyes he meant the night itself.

"Yes, it is, of course it is, a special night, and everything is so beautiful – the music, the decorations, all the wonderful guests."

"What else could the night be but beautiful when you are the one gracing it with your presence?"

Sarah half-grinned and shook her head. "Oh, Malcolm what shall I do with you? You burst upon my life like an artillery shell from one of uncle's cannons and you are saying things no one has been so bold to say my entire life, let alone the evening of my eighteenth birthday. I'm supposed to know who you are but you are nothing like the boy I last saw in 1857. You might as well be the man in the moon you are such a stranger to me."

"I don't wish to remain a stranger."

"And I confess I don't wish you to either. But who are you, Malcolm Becket Ross, how can you have changed so much from the child you used to be?"

"Why, I grew up, Miss Sarah, just like you did. It's just that I had a lot more growing up to do than you. Your uncle helped with that quite a bit. Drill, drill, drill. Pray, pray, pray. Haul the cannons around like a team of horses. Load, aim, fire. Rain or shine. Eat what's put before you and thank God. March, present arms, march again. I had no time to be a child anymore. I left him on a muddy field in Lexington three and a half years ago."

"Oh." She paused in her dancing. "The music's stopped."

"Do we need it?"

She smiled at the flash and sparkle in his blue eyes. "I guess not."

He continued to move her around the room while everyone stood still and watched, the violins silent. She thought she would be embarrassed but she didn't feel a thing, smiling up at the face of a stranger she had known since age five yet she didn't know at all except that whoever and whatever he had become was pleasant to hold and be held by. The flags and faces and candle flames were a blur as he waltzed her from one end of the room to the other and back again, the only sounds his breath and hers, the swish of her gown, the snap and slide of his leather boots over the brightly polished floor. Then as if the bandleader had finally realized what was going on in front of his eyes he swung his baton and the musicians struck up a tune and others began to dance alongside Sarah and Malcolm again. Sarah made a face without meaning to.

"What's wrong?" asked Malcolm quickly. "Did I do something?"

"No, no, I just liked the silence, that's all. It was kind of magical dancing like that."

"If you like we could step outside and dance under the stars."

"Just the two of us?"

"Just the two of us."

"You are bold."

"If I am it's your uncle who made me that way. I really was Malcolm the Mouse until he got ahold of me."

"Yes, well, we certainly can't call you that anymore. I really don't think you are Malcolm Becket Ross, to tell you the truth. I shall have to give you a new name."

"What will it be?"

"Malcolm the Mighty?" She put a hand over her lips as they danced. "That sounds as funny as Malcolm the Mouse." She smiled at him as the band continued to play. "Malcolm the Marksman – are you any good at shooting a musket? Malcolm the Meteor?"

They both laughed.

Then he pulled her closer so that the smile left her face with one look at the intensity in his.

"You could try Malcolm the Man," he said quietly. "How does that sound?"

She said nothing as they waltzed.

"Dance with me outside?" he asked again.

"I know," she replied. "You will soon be leaving to go and fight a war for me."

"No. I will soon be leaving so that I can come back again."

"Is that what's on your mind? Are you sure it isn't grand parades or pretty girls throwing flowers or a kiss from every belle in Virginia?"

The blue in his eyes suddenly became as dark as an evening sky. "I'd take one kiss from Sarah Felicity Nunley over a thousand from the women of Richmond. I've wanted to kiss Sarah Nunley since I was seven years old. Do you remember that pony race our families took us to in Winchester?"

She barely recalled it. "Yes."

'That's when it all started for me. Right then and there once the wind plucked the bonnet from your head and all your hair unraveled in the sunlight. Yes, I was only seven but I felt like I was twenty-one." He whirled her so that her gown flew through the air like a wave. "Please dance outside with me, Sarah, even if it's just for one minute, one half minute. Please." A smile slid over his lips. "After all, I am going to war for you, aren't I?"

The waltz ended and the bandleader spoke up. "Ladies and gentlemen, Major Jackson has informed me the time has come when our brave soldiers must carry on to Richmond, but before they go, please join with me in wishing them God speed and singing them a rousing chorus of Dixie."

Several banjos appeared from among the band members and the tune was swiftly on its way.

I wish I was in the land of cotton
Old times they are not forgotten
Look away! Look away! Look away! Dixie Land

In Dixie Land where I was born
Early on one frosty morn,
Look away! Look away! Look away! Dixie Land

Oh I wish I was in Dixie, away, away
In Dixie Land I'll make my stand
Away down south in Dixie
Away, away, away down south in Dixie
Away, away, away down south in Dixie

Uncle Thomas swept his blue forage cap from his head. "I thank you on behalf of the men and the Institute for your hospitality!" he boomed. "Now I must ask my Virginians to pick up whatever equipment they have left on the porch and form ranks for the march to the railroad station. A train is waiting there to take us the rest of the way to the capital. I wish my niece every blessing in our Lord Jesus Christ and I hope you will pray for our boys as they prepare to defend your homes and plantations from the enemy."

He returned the cap to his head and strode through the ballroom doors to the main entryway. The cadets bowed to their partners, set down their punch glasses, and scrambled after him. Sarah's father gave her mother a kiss on the cheek, adjusted the sword on his belt, gestured to his sons, and followed the crowd of gray uniforms out of the room. Malcolm half-smiled at Sarah and shrugged.

"Well, I tried to get you out under the stars, Sarah Felicity Nunley."

He bowed, squared his shoulders, and walked away.

What do I say? I don't even know what just happened. Who is he? What is he?

"Malcolm."

He stopped and glanced back.

"Malcolm. Please call again."

He smiled. "If I don't get shot."

"Make up your mind not to get shot."

"I'll do my best."

Sarah joined her mother and they went out to the porch together. Lanterns gleamed on the grass and on the dirt lane that wound up to their house through the oak trees. The cadets and older men like her father had already formed a column and begun the short march to the station, two men shoulder to shoulder, one pair after another. Over a dozen young men who were wearing their best suits for the ball fell into step with them. The tramp of feet was louder than the music that started to drift out from the ballroom.

"Mama." Sarah noticed the sharp lines around her mother's eyes and mouth. "Please don't fret." She put her arm about her mother's waist. "States fighting states? Brother against brother? American against American? It can't last long."

"It's nice to think so. But your father was gone for almost two years over that awful war with Mexico. It was a dreadful worry."

"But this is a quarrel amongst ourselves. An American family squabble. I don't believe we will still be at it six months from now let alone two years."

Mrs. Nunley grasped her daughter's free hand. "I hope you're right." She patted Sarah's arm. "Let's go back inside. There are no more butterflies left but perhaps you can enjoy a waltz with an old timer like Mr. Jacobs."

"Butterflies? What ever do you mean?"

"Well, what else should I call a caterpillar that crawled away into his cocoon and came out looking like Malcolm Becket Ross?"

"Oh." Sarah's cheeks warmed. "It was a rather shocking transformation, I agree. I don't know what to make of him. Honestly, I feel like I was run over by a carriage."

They went back to the ballroom, arm in arm.

"You can be grateful he's out of your life for a few months," said her mother. "You have a chance to catch your breath. It appeared to me you had very little of it left."

"What?" Sarah's face burned. "Did our dancing look scandalous to you?"

"Scandalous? Oh, my goodness, not at all. It was quite wonderful to watch. Really the best thing for a coming of age ball. A dash of romance."

"Romance? Mama, I hardly know him."

"Nonsense. You grew up together."

"That was – that was – another Malcolm altogether. I don't know this one at all."

"Well, now you have plenty of time to think about him."

"Think? I don't know what to think," moaned Sarah. "I was having such a splendid time and now I feel wretched."

"Do you?" Her mother smiled. "I'm sure old Mr. Jacobs can set things to rights again. He's a fine dancer and he'll whisk you across the room."

"I don't want to be whisked."

"Of course you do."

"Certainly not by Mr. Jacobs. He must be a hundred years old."

"Fifty, my dear, fifty. He's just what you need right now. He'll be a tonic."

"I'm not interested in tonics or whisking."

"Cheer up. You'll have plenty of time to mull over the mystery of the caterpillar and the butterfly when you're alone in your bedroom."

Sarah mulled a great deal once she lay in her bed in the dark. She missed the sound of her father walking through the house in the noisy boots mother always wanted him to remove at the door. And though her brothers had been away at the Institute for years the few hours they'd been with her again made their fresh loss sharp. She avoided thoughts of Malcolm Becket Ross as long as she could, praying for her mother's health and the safety of her father and brothers, but eventually the bewildering events of the evening forced their way to the front of her mind.

I was enjoying the ball until this tall young man with perfect hair and perfect skin stepped through the doors and wretched Christopher Scott Nunley beckoned him over.

She could feel the muscles of his back under her fingers. The gentle strength that held her hand. Breath from a mouth that had taken in coffee and bread and wild honey. The scent of rain from his uniform and a soap with mint in it from his face. A smile that lit wicks in her.

Oh, for heaven's sakes, Sarah Nunley, stop this. A man doesn't just waltz into your life and turn you inside out. You're made of sterner stuff. If he's been molded by your uncle, why, so have you, and for a much longer period of time. He's gone off to that silly war and you won't see him again. He'll find a bride in Richmond and you'll find a groom from one of the plantations and you won't have to think about him again.

"But perhaps he'll write," she said out loud. "He could. Just a note. He knows where I live."

The note when it came was not from Malcolm Becket Ross, it was from his commanding officer, her uncle.

June 29
My dear Sarah
I meant to write much sooner but a great deal has been going on from day to day. I will not say where I am, or give the names or

numbers of any of the regiments, but I can tell you the Virginians have been placed under my command and God has been pleased to raise me to the rank of brigadier general. I told my mi bella esposa Mary Ann that it was more than I expected but I shall endeavor to make good my God and my country's trust in me.

Now of course your father and brothers are in one of my regiments. I tell them nothing for I do not want it to go to their heads but they have turned into fine soldiers, practically flawless in drill, in marksmanship, and in general discipline and military ardor. The enemy shall hear from your family soon enough. I doubt not but that your father will be promoted to major very soon. However do not tell your mother all this; it will only make her fret more.

That is all I have time to tell you. Pray for us. The summer will not pass before there is a major battle so bring your uncle and brothers and father before the throne of grace at every opportunity.

I remain your Old Uncle Thomas though I feel less old and far more vigorous since the war has begun. Being in the field since April agrees with me.

She had only tucked the note away in a drawer in her vanity for a few weeks when news came of a great battle in northern Virginia. But everything she heard was garbled. Billy King said the field slaves and household slaves had heard two different stories – in one the North had routed the South and in the other the South had won and was marching on Washington. Some newspapers at first warned of disaster while others threw caution to the wind and heralded a victory. Her mother paced the kitchen for thirty or forty minutes at a time.

"I'm sure we've won, Mother," Sarah tried to soothe her. "All the papers are saying the same thing today. That's what Malcolm's father came by to tell me."

"The war isn't over with one battle, my dear," her mother replied in a soft voice. "The next one could be tomorrow or the day after."

"Perhaps the Yankees have had enough."

"The Yankees will have enough when they've beaten us into the ground, Sarah. They are tenacious as bulldogs."

"I will hope for the best."

Her mother gave Sarah a half smile. "Of course you will." She continued to pace the kitchen. "How many battles there are doesn't concern me. It's what happens to your father and brothers. Sometimes I pray they will get wounded, each one of them, wounded so badly they cannot fight again and have to be sent home."

"Mama! What a terrible thing to pray for! Suppose Warren lost an arm or papa both his legs?"

"Ah, don't worry, my dear. Prayer is not magic. I can't make God do my bidding. He will not answer prayers he considers wrong or wicked just because I prayed them." She moaned as she walked. "Women from the North or the South just want the same thing – their loved ones to return home safe. But that can't be when it comes to a war, it can never be. Some of us will lose our sons and husbands and uncles. Already many have lost those they prayed they would never lose. What the papers in Richmond call a great victory is not a great victory to the woman who has lost the love of her life."

The morning after her mother had said this Sarah was sitting on the porch reading her Bible. It was the first of August and only a light breeze gave any relief from the heat. She heard the sound of a horse walking, its hooves snapping against the earth and stone of their drive. Looking up she saw a rider in gray uniform emerge from the oaks that grew on other side of the path.

"Malcolm!" She got to her feet, a surge of excitement and surprise cutting through her along with a stab of confusion. "What are you doing here? Is the war over?"

He stopped his chestnut at the front of the house and looked up at her. "We licked them. But it's not over. They'll be back. Or we'll go to them."

"I heard you marched on Washington."

A smile came and went on Malcolm's face. "That's what your uncle wanted to do. He was ready to charge after the bluecoats. *Give me ten thousand men!* But beating them wasn't that easy, Miss Sarah. And it wouldn't have been a church picnic taking Washington." His young face darkened so that to Sarah he looked ten years older. "War isn't what we thought. It isn't like being on parade or singing Dixie." He looked over her shoulder. "Where's Mrs. Nunley? Where's your mother?"

"I'm not sure."

"I need to see her. They sent me here to see her."

"Who sent you?"

"General Jackson, your uncle. My captain and lieutenant too."

"Why?"

"I'll tell you when she's here with you."

Sarah glanced into the house and saw Letta. "Go fetch Mrs. Nunley as quickly as you can."

"Yes, Miss Sarah. I believe she's walking in the forest behind the house."

Malcolm did not dismount. His eyes were on Sarah but she felt no warmth from them, only a chill that made the heat of the morning feel like December. Finally she looked down at the boards of the porch under her feet.

"They were driving us." She looked back up when he spoke. "Don't y'all believe the Richmond newspapers. The Yankees were pouring over us. Your uncle had us crouching low, the Virginians, and he was sitting on that horse of his we call Little Sorrel, Minie balls slicing up the air all around him. He didn't flinch. So one of the other generals starts yelling about your uncle sitting there like a stone wall – I don't know if he was admiring his courage or cussing him because he wouldn't move the Virginians forward into the fight. But as soon as the Yankees were on top of us your uncle had us jump to our feet and shoot all at once and the Yankees went down like cut wheat. Then we screamed like a pack of demons and went at them with bayonets fixed. They fell back and we got in among them and it was hand to hand fighting for an hour, fists and musket stocks and knives and shooting men only a foot in front of your face. In the end they broke and ran and their whole army kind of lost their heads and tore back to Washington as fast as they could go. That's how we won. Just about the time we almost lost." The smile came and went again. "They are calling your uncle Stonewall now. Stonewall Jackson. I have letters from him for you and your mother."

"Stonewall Jackson." Sarah repeated the name as she stared at Malcolm. "You haven't said a thing about my father and brothers."

"What is it?" Sarah's mother hurried out of the house with Letta behind her. "Why are you here, Master Ross? What news have you brought us?"

Malcolm hesitated, looking at her. Then he dismounted and stood by his horse, holding its reins in his hand. He took his cap off his head.

"Ma'am, Mrs. Nunley." He hesitated again. "I'm sorry, ma'am. I have been sent to tell you in person that your husband fell in battle and is buried near Bull Run Creek with the other Virginians. A lot of our boys went down. I'm sorry, so sorry, Mrs. Nunley, Miss Sarah."

Sarah and her mother had their hands over their mouths. Mrs. Nunley leaned her weight against her daughter.

"What about my sons?" Mrs. Nunley could barely speak. "What can you tell me about my sons?"

"They are wounded."

"All of them?"

"Yes, ma'am. But they are recovering. No amputations, no infection. They will be back in the ranks again in a month or less."

Mrs. Nunley began to waver. Sarah threw an arm around her waist.

"I am instructed to offer you the condolences of General Jackson and the other officers serving in Captain Nunley's regiment. He fought bravely and was always there at the side of his men. His loss is greatly mourned. The captain was particularly kind to me and I mourn his death as much as anyone in our army. He was a great man and a great Virginian."

Mrs. Nunley collapsed so suddenly Sarah could not hold her. She struck her head against the porch railing and blood darted over her forehead. Sarah screamed and the slaves and Malcolm came running. Malcolm put his arms under Mrs. Nunley's shoulders and Billy King grasped her by the feet while Letta and Harriet smoothed down her dress.

"Where can we take her?" Malcolm asked Sarah.

"Up to her room, please, up to her room and lay her on her bed." Sarah turned to another male slave. "Tommy, you take old Cob and you get to Doc Parker's and you tell him what's happened and get him to come quickly."

"Yes, Miss Sarah."

Sarah walked beside her mother as Malcolm and Billy King carried her up the staircase, holding one of her hands and patting it. "Mama. Mama. Wake up. Wake up, please."

She pushed open the door to the room and Malcolm and Billy King laid Mrs. Nunley as gently as they could on her large bed. Sarah bent over her mother and listened for her breathing. Then she put a hand over her mother's heart. She wiped tears out of her eyes with the fingers of her free hand and pulled away.

"I can't feel anything and I can't hear anything."

"Let me listen, Miss Sarah," said Letta. "Let's all be real quiet, real quiet."

Letta leaned over Mrs. Nunley and put her ear to the woman's mouth. Harriet rushed in with a basin of water and a cloth and began to wipe away the blood on Mrs. Nunely's face, smoothing back her hair as she did so. Letta continued to listen as if Harriet was not there. Sarah stood back and watched, running her fingers over her eyes again and again. Letta moved her head and put her ear to Mrs. Nunley's chest. Then she straightened and took Sarah's hands in hers.

"Have the soldier listen, Miss Sarah."

"Why? Can't you tell how she is?"

"He's been on the battlefield. His ears is younger and sharper than mine and he's been on the battlefield and listened for other men's breaths and other men's heart's beating. Have the soldier listen."

Sarah turned her swollen eyes on Malcolm. "Could you, please?"

"Miss Sarah, I don't have any special skills, I'm not a surgeon."

"Please. I don't know what I'm hearing or not hearing. I'm too distraught."

Malcolm went to the bed and stood looking down at Mrs. Nunley's white face. Then he knelt by the bed and took her hand in one of his, put his ear by her lips a long time, kept his fingers on her wrist. He did not say anything.

"Malcolm." Sarah's voice was a whisper. "Malcolm, please."

He did not look at her but put his hand on the damp forehead Harriet had washed clean. It looked to Sarah as if he were praying as he ran his hand slowly over her mother's brow.

"It's not my way to come to a home and bring them hard news of a loved one's death," Malcolm said, keeping his eyes on Sarah's mother. "It's not my way to do it more than once. There's no heartbeat. There's no breath. God forgive me. God forgive me, Sarah. There's no breath."

The Storm

The rain was pounding on the roof and cracking against the windows as if the Union army had surrounded Seven Oaks and opened fire.

Sarah lay in her bed thinking.

Her mother had been in her grave a week. Grief over losing both her mother and father drove her to her knees whenever she went into her room and shut the door. But the running of the plantation made her stand like iron whenever she gave orders to the field slaves and household slaves. It had been a difficult transition to make, one moment the doting daughter and belle of the mansion, the next the mistress of Seven Oaks with no men to around to rely on.

Except Malcolm Beckett Ross.

"I would not have made it through the first week without him, would I, Lord?" she said out loud.

She watched the rain slide down the windowpane. The mixture of light and darkness, the green of the trees, and the movement of the raindrops combined to create an image of Malcolm's face.

"He stood by my side at the funeral. Helped me address the slaves those first few days. Wrote Uncle Thomas for permission to stay on longer with the passing of my mother. Has listened to me day in and day out and accompanied me on all my weeks and rides about the plantation."

She sat up in her nightgown and touched the glass pane with her fingers.

What a surprise you have turned out to be. An officer and a gentleman. A Southern girl's dream. Riding here every day from your parents' mansion. Refusing to stay overnight so that tongues would not wag. But today is your last visit. You are heading back to your Virginians. Back to the war we thought would be so heroic and wonderful. What if a Yankee bullet finds you like it found my father?

She wrapped her arms around her knees.

"I can't let myself love you, Malcolm," she whispered. "I see the way you look at me but I cannot rest my eyes on you in that way. I cannot offer you any passion. If it were peacetime, oh, I would flirt with you outrageously and use all the charms Virginia has taught me to nurture and make use of. But I could lose my brothers, every one of them. Suppose I lost you as well after giving you my heart? I can't risk it. I'm so sorry. You're like a shooting star and you've lit up my night. But a heart can only be broken so many times before it stops working. I can't let myself love you, sweet Malcolm Beckett Ross. I can't."

There was rapping on the door.

"Yes, I'm up, thank you, Letta," she said.

"Miss Sarah. Malcolm Beckett Ross is here."

"So soon? We normally don't see him till ten or eleven."

"The rivers and creeks are flooding, Miss Sarah. I don't know how he got over them. He's in a terrible state. Billy King had to help him off his horse."

"What?" Sarah threw off her quilt and jumped out of bed. "Letta, come in here. You must help me get dressed as quickly as possible."

Letta opened the door and rushed to Sarah's closet.

"Where does Billy King have him now, Letta?"

"In the parlor in front of a hot fire."

"Not in his wet clothing?"

"No, Miss Sarah. Billy took his uniform to Harriet to wash clean and dry out. It was covered in mud. Why, it was even torn in a few places. He mumbled that he was clean swept away once or twice."

"Swept away?" Sarah had her hoop skirt and corset on and lifted her arms for Letta to drop a pale green dress over her. "How did he make it out of the floods then?"

"He says he never lost his grip on his horse's reins. His horse kept a-swimming and pulled Master Ross out of everything."

"Get Tommy to take special care of that horse. Rubbed down, in the stalls, a blanket, oats, everything."

"Yes, Miss Sarah."

Sarah looked at herself in the mirror and fidgeted while Letta worked on her hair.

"What is the horse's name?" she demanded.

"Jupiter, I believes."

"Double the oats for Jupiter."

"Yes, Miss Sarah."

"He is a big strong horse."

"Eighteen hands, yes."

"That is why Master Ross is still alive."

"I believes so."

And that is why I cannot give you my heart, Malcolm. How easily it could have been broken again today.

Sarah hurried down the staircase ahead of Letta.

"What has Billy dressed him in?" she asked as she descended the spiral staircase.

"Some blankets, Miss Sarah."

"Blankets? I am sure they warmed him up but I cannot possibly converse with him in blankets. Have Billy bring him some clean clothes."

"Whose?"

"Whose? I don't know whose!" Sarah thought a moment as she stood in the hallway. "Warren and him are about the same height and build, aren't they?"

"Well, yes, Miss Sarah, but Master Ross does have broader shoulders and another three inches on your brother."

"We have to dress him in something."

"Christopher has shot up and put on good weight, Miss Sarah. He did bring some civilian clothing home with him from the Institute."

"All right. Fine. Fetch pants and a shirt and coat and shoes from Christopher's closet. Have Billy King get them on Malcolm. Or is he fit to dress himself?"

"I don't know. We had to close a nasty cut across his forehead with a tight cloth. He bled through two of them."

"What? What else haven't you told me?"

"There were cuts all over his legs and arms as well. It was like he came off of a battlefield, I swear."

Sarah looked at the parlor door. It was shut tight.

"Why on earth did he come here when there was such a bad storm and with the rivers swollen and all?"

Letta dropped her eyes. "He came for you, Miss Sarah. I don't have to tell you that."

Sarah felt a sudden flush spring onto her face.

She waved her hand in the air. "Go fetch the set of clothing and give it to Billy King."

"Yes, Miss Sarah."

Sarah paced up and down the hallway while Billy King got Malcolm into a set of Christopher's civilian clothes.

I gave you no reason to hope for anything. You knew I was well settled into my role as mistress of the plantation. Why did you take such a risk? I haven't promised a thing.

Billy King poked his head out of the parlor. "He's presentable, Miss Sarah."

"Thank you, Billy. Does he have fresh coffee?"

"Yes, Miss."

"Something hot to eat?"

"Not yet."

"Bring a plate from the kitchen for myself and Master Ross. Triple the portions on his plate."

"Yes, Miss."

Sarah whisked into the room.

Malcolm was sitting in a chair with the door to the woodstove open and sparks snapping onto the heavy socks on his feet. A white bandage with a bloodspot circled his head just below his hairline. Black and purple splotches marked both sides of his face. He smiled at her.

"Miss Nunley."

Her hands were on her hips. "Malcolm Beckett Ross, what were you thinking? You could have been killed."

"I swear I didn't know the creeks and rivers were that bad."

"Well, once you saw that they were you should have turned back."

"I licked the first flood so I reckoned I could lick the others too."

"You reckoned? Is this how you conduct yourself in battle too?"

"If I do I learned it from your uncle."

Sarah walked to the large windows and watched the trees bend in the wind and rain. Then she whirled to face him again.

"You see why I can't possibly fall in love with you?"

"What?"

"You're reckless. Careless. You'd toss away your life just to keep a promise to a lady."

"Not any lady. To you."

"It doesn't matter who you make your promises to. You shouldn't throw yourself into a raging river to keep them. Or hurl yourself against a line of Yankee cannon."

"You need me here, Sarah."

"I don't need you here, Malcolm Beckett Ross. I never gave you the impression I did."

"Not in so many words."

"Not in any words at all. We are friends, good friends, you were a wonderful assistance to me the week after my mother's death, in every respect conducting yourself like a gentleman, a Christian, and a true Virginian. But that's all, Malcolm. That's all. I don't need you plunging to your death on account of me. I am not your lady, I am not your lover, never, never, can I be either of those."

"I see." Malcolm pushed himself to his feet.

"What are you doing?" she asked.

"I will need my boots and my uniform. I trust Jupiter is in the stables?"

"Yes, he's in the stables. But you can't ride him in this storm."

"Of course I can."

"Are you thinking of heading back home? That's absurd. The rivers are still running over their banks."

"I'm heading back to my regiment. You don't need me. But my country does."

"Any of the creeks and streams between here and the army will be just as bad or worse than the ones you almost drowned in to get to Seven Oaks."

Malcolm walked to the door. "I made it, didn't I? I'll make it to my regiment as well."

He opened the door. She rushed over, slammed it shut, and leaned her back against it.

"You're not going through this door, Malcolm Beckett Ross."

"Step aside, please, Miss Sarah."

"Don't call me Miss Sarah. I am not stepping aside. I am not going anywhere. Neither are you."

"Miss Sarah, I have a duty; I have an obligation."

Her face was dark red. "Not to get killed you don't."

His was darker and redder. "Yes, to get killed if it comes to that. That is part of my oath. Now step aside, please, Miss Sarah."

"What about your obligation to me?"

"I don't have an obligation to you. Or if I did it's come to an end."

"Just like that?"

"Yes, just like that. You spoke the words yourself."

"I didn't."

"You did."

"I just meant – "

He cut her off. "You were perfectly clear about what you meant. Now if you don't step aside I shall have to physically remove you."

"You wouldn't dare."

"If I need to remove you so I can get to my horse and my regiment I will most certainly dare."

"I'd like to see you try."

"Miss Sarah – "

"Stop Miss Sarah'ing me, Malcolm Beckett Ross! You'll go out from under my roof when I say so and not a minute before!"

"Is that so? You have Irish blood, didn't you tell me that once?"

"So what if I do?" snapped Sarah.

"I have some myself. And a good dash of Scot."

"That makes no difference to me. It doesn't change anything."

"It makes a difference to what's going to happen next."

"Nothing is going to happen next except you're going to sit back down and get away from this door."

Malcolm suddenly swung her up in his arms and carried her to the other side of the room.

"What are you doing?" She kicked out with her legs. "Put me down!"

"I won't."

She slapped him across the face. "You will!"

"I won't."

She slapped him again.

Fresh blood darted out from under the bandage wrapped around his head.

"Oh, no!" She tried to wipe away the blood with her fingers. "Malcolm, I'm so sorry, I've opened the wound again, oh, Malcolm, forgive me."

Their faces were close together as she frantically struck at the blood flow.

She looked in his eyes. "Malcolm, are you all right?"

The blue in them was intense.

"I am," he replied, keeping his eyes on hers.

Her face came even closer as she rubbed at a streak of blood with her thumb.

"I think it's stopped," she said.

"Sorry to hear it."

"What do you mean? Are you the sort of person who likes to bleed?"

"I'm the sort of person who likes your fingers touching his face."

The blue seemed to take her out of herself and completely inside of him.

"We can't, Malcolm," she said.

"What can't we?"

"Fall in love. Kiss. Embrace."

"Why not?"

"It would kill me if something happened to you."

"It would kill me if something didn't happen between you and me."

Her hand wiped at another spot of blood on his face and stopped.

"We can't." She could not pull herself away from the vivid blue of his eyes. "We mustn't."

"I think we must."

"Why do you think that?"

"If something did happen to me or to you and we'd never kissed and the other was left with that kind of emptiness it would be a sin."

"A sin?"

"And no sin is good. It's better to kiss, Sarah Felicity Nunley, than upset the Almighty."

A smile found its way onto her face. She ran her hand gently over his skin.

"When did you become such a smooth talker?" she asked. "When did you become such a Southern gentleman?"

"When did you become such a beauty?"

"Don't say those things."

"Of course I'll say those things. Do you want me to add lies to my sin of not kissing you? Do you want me to say you have no beauty at all when it was the Almighty who gave you your beauty? I expect he would be greatly offended."

She continued to caress his face. "No one should offend the Lord."

"I agree."

"But Malcolm – "

Sarah could not finish her sentence. His lips brushed against hers and it felt to Sarah like a rocket had burst in her head. Her whole body jumped. His lips closed on hers with warmth and strength and he pulled her against his chest while he held her off the floor and cradled her in his arms.

She tugged herself free of the kiss and protested, "Malcolm, we shouldn't."

"We must. Before God Almighty, we must."

"No more nonsense. I'm mistress of this plantation now. I need to behave myself. I need to act in keeping with the decorum expected of a lady of my position."

His lips gently found her neck and throat and shoulder.

Her body jumped again.

The fingers of both hands curled themselves in his shining black hair.

She threw her head back and closed her eyes as he continued to touch his mouth to her face and cheeks.

"Oh, Malcolm."

It was Sarah who finally yanked his head up, tugging him by the black hair wrapped in her fingers, and brought his mouth down on hers again, putting all her heat and passion and power into the kiss, lacing both arms around his neck and bringing him in so close she could not breathe and did not care.

"Thank goodness," he finally said, his breath coming in short bursts.

"Thank goodness for what?"

"We have thwarted sin."

His kisses came again and again so that she could not reply but only hang on and return them.

"Besides all your joking," she whispered, lifting her lips from his, "what does all this mean?"

A knock sounded on the door.

"Miss Sarah." It was Billy King. "I have your breakfast here, yours and the special plate for Master Ross."

"Special plate?" asked Malcolm.

"Just leave it at the door, please, Billy, and thank you."

"Yes, Miss Sarah."

"Special plate?" Malcolm asked again.

"Just more biscuits and gravy than I have on mine."

She smiled, her arms still around his neck, his arms still holding her up off the floor and against his chest, his own smile as rich and warm as hers.

The storm had grown fierce. Tree branches slashed the tall windowpanes of the parlor.

Malcolm glanced at the wood stove. "The fire is going out."

Her smile deepened and her fingers wound themselves in his hair again. "Not this fire."

"True. And it's the only fire I need."

"Don't just say that."

"I'm not just saying that."

"Aren't you tired of holding me?"

"No."

"Your arms must be worn out."

"Never."

She laughed. "You can't be that strong. Everyone gets tired."

"I am that strong and I feel no fatigue whatsoever."

"Be honest."

"I swear. I can do this all day."

"I thought you were weak from fighting your way through the floods to get to me."

"I never said I was weak. It was your people who trussed me up like a prize turkey."

"So how are you prepared to spend the rest of this storm day?"

"I'm happy where I am."

"The lady of the plantation has to make her appearance at some point. Storm or not I have to get the household ready for winter. We don't have enough firewood for one thing."

"I'd be happy to supervise that."

"And the smokehouse is near empty. Hogs need to be butchered."

"I can supervise that as well. Just as I do at home."

"I'm sorry we have no venison."

"I enjoy the hunt."

"Not in this weather."

"Once the storm abates and before I return to my regiment."

She pouted. "Do you have to return to your regiment?"

"You know I do. I serve Virginia. We both do."

An impulse came over her.

He saw light flicker in her deep brown eyes.

"What's come over you?" he asked.

"Let's see how long I can get you to stay," she murmured and nuzzled his neck.

"Do you want me to be shot for desertion?"

"Oh, Uncle Thomas wouldn't shoot my beau. Horsewhip you perhaps." She unbound her brown and auburn hair with one hand, pins dropping on the hardwood floor, and with the other caressed his face, continuing to nuzzle and kiss his neck while she pressed her small white teeth softly against his ear. "Wouldn't it be worth it?"

He closed his eyes and held her more tightly as she kissed him.

"I believe you are right. It would be worth it."

"So perhaps you could stay another week. Or month. Or until Christmas."

"Then I really would be shot, beau or no beau."

"But it would be a sin not to linger here, wouldn't it? I can give you such memories to go back to the army with."

He sighed. "I already have such memories. I am receiving them now."

She turned her head so that her hair fell over his face and chest.

"I can give you more, Malcolm."

"You really are a temptress, aren't you, behind your quiet eyes and smiles?"

"If I am then I'm a temptress to do what is good and noble and right. Stay with me longer, Malcolm. I need you."

"You said you didn't need me."

"That was my game. This is not. I need you."

"I'll stay as long as duty permits."

"Will you write my uncle another letter?" She kept on kissing his neck, moving her lips up and down the side of his face. "Will you write one soon?"

"I'll write it today. If I ever decide to put you down."

"We can't get it to the post office today."

"I'll write it today and post it tomorrow."

"The river and creeks will still be high tomorrow."

"No matter."

"Through storm and flood to ask leave to remain with a Southern lady in distress."

"They may send cavalry to fetch me back. They may send Jeb Stuart."

Malcolm suddenly placed her on her feet.

She staggered at the rapid change from being in his arms to standing upright on the floor.

"Why did you do that, Malcolm? What's wrong?"

He took her hand and pulled her down behind a sofa.

"Yankee troopers!" he hissed.

She followed his eyes and saw ten or eleven men in blue on horseback, hunched over in the wind and rain, hog carcasses tied down onto a half dozen of the saddles.

"They must be raiders," muttered Malcolm. "Sent behind our army to cut up railroad tracks and telegraph lines. I expect they've snuck up the Shenandoah Valley."

"Why are they out in such weather?"

"It's perfect weather for working mischief."

"The cowards!"

"Hush. We do the same thing." Malcolm tracked the troopers' movements. "They've broken into your smokehouse. Now it looks like they're headed for the stables."

"They'll steal our horses."

"That is their intention." He spotted a musket on the wall above a bookcase. "Is that thing loaded?"

"Papa kept all the firearms loaded. He changed the powder and shot every month."

Malcolm crept to the bookcase, stood up quickly and grasped the musket, then crouched again.

"Do you permit your slaves to handle guns?" he asked Sarah.

"Only if we have trouble with poachers or varmints."

"Does Billy King know where the other muskets are?"

"Yes. So do I for that matter. Papa taught me how to shoot. I'm not a helpless girl."

Malcolm smiled. "I don't think I ever thought that."

"It's good you didn't."

"So I need you to get muskets in the hands of Billy King and Tommy and any other slaves you trust, men or women. I need them to be ready to fire once I fire. We only have a few minutes."

"Where shall we shoot from?"

"The windows. Get everyone else out of the way and into the rooms at the back of the house."

"I will."

Malcolm put a hand on her arm.

"What is it?" she asked.

"You be careful. All of you be careful."

"Of course we will."

"You've talked a lot about losing me. Well, I don't want to lose you either. You make me feel like a hawk."

"A hawk?"

"So strong. So free. Yes."

A smile came back to her face. "I'm glad of that. If you mean it."

"I do mean it."

"This is the only good day I've had since the death of my father and mother. I would like it to stay a good day, Malcolm. So if I must watch myself so must you."

"I promise." He squeezed her arm gently. "Bring me a powder horn and more shot as soon as you can."

"No need. Papa has all of that stashed in the drawer of the desk in the corner. And caps to ignite the charge too."

She was out the door, bent over so the Union cavalrymen could not see her.

Malcolm crawled to the desk. Each drawer was locked.

Lord God, no. I've got to have more than one shot.

He glanced up. The troopers had moved well away from the windows and the house and had gathered by the stables. He slammed the butt of the musket against the first locked drawer several times. The drawer finally fell open but there were only papers inside. The second drawer only held knives. When he smashed the lock on the third drawer he was finally rewarded with a large powder horn, caps to go on the nipple of the musket and ignite the powder in the barrel, and a bag of large lead balls. The horn had a strap and he slung it over his shoulder. Then he crawled to the windows with the musket in one hand and the caps and balls in the other. He opened one of the tall windows by unlatching it and slowly pushing it to the right. Rain struck his face and hand.

"Steady, Scotty. Lead him out. He's a beauty. Full of spirit."

Malcolm heard the voice clearly.

A trooper was tugging Jupiter out of the stables. He'd put the bit in the horse's mouth and saddled him but the gelding was not happy and kept pulling back on the reins. The trooper was on foot and began to slip and slide in the mud.

"Are there are any other horses worth the effort?" asked the officer.

"Aye," responded Scotty. "A couple of blacks."

"Henderson. Billings. Go fetch them."

"What about the house, captain?"

"Leave the house alone. Our orders are not to molest civilians in any way."

Malcolm cocked the musket, put a cap on the nipple, and rose to his knees, aiming at the trooper named Scotty who had Jupiter by the reins. There was no clear shot so he lowered the musket and waited.

There will be a better opportunity. Sarah and the others will need more time anyways.

He leaned his back against the wall.

Getting to Seven Oaks that morning had been one of the most frightening experiences of his life. Several times he was certain the floodwaters would take him and every time Jupiter had pulled him to the other bank. Why he had been so determined to get to Sarah Felicity Nunley he still was not sure. Her sudden kisses had been a complete surprise. If he'd been in church he'd have been more than ready to thank God and sing every hymn the minister announced with as much enthusiasm and volume as he could muster. Of course she could change her mind by that evening and never want to kiss him again.

Well, even if she doesn't kiss me again, and even if her uncle has my head for breakfast, I'm going to make sure Sarah's ready for winter and has her slaves in hand. I won't head back to the regiment until I feel confident about her situation here. If I can't do that without getting court martialed what's the point of fighting for Virginia at all?

In the kitchen, which had several windows that faced towards the stables, Sarah had shooed out everyone but herself, Tommy, and Billy King. Each of them had two muskets, one in their hands, one leaning against the wall next to where they crouched. Tommy and Billy had tried to argue Sarah out of getting involved with the shooting but hadn't gotten very far.

"You could get hit, Miss Sarah," Billy protested.

"I don't believe I will."

"Glass will be flying."

"A few bits of broken glass won't bother me."

"Let me at least get Jimmy Buck and Cleveland up from the slaves' quarters."

"No. That's too far away. And even if you go out by the back door the Yankees are sure to spot you and run you down. Besides, Jimmy and Cleveland never get a day of rest but for Sundays. Let them be. The three of us and Master Ross are all we need to handle those troopers."

"Lord, your mama or papa wouldn't want to see y'all in this situation."

"Well, they're not here to fret about it, Billy King."

"Your brothers wouldn't like it."

"And they're not here either, are they? So stop arguing with me, Billy King, and crack the windows open. I don't want to miss the sound of Master Ross's shot."

"Why, he's in the front parlor. We're bound to hear the boom of the musket even with the windows shut and our hands over our ears."

"Open them just the same. It'll keep you from talking and you won't be able to quarrel with me anymore." She smiled. "What are you worried about? Didn't you always say I was a tomboy?"

Billy King smiled back. "Not since you growed up into a fine young woman. Nows I'm afraid the tomboy in you has come back and made y'all into a firebrand."

"Thank you. I take that as a compliment. I don't mind being a Southern firebrand. Virginia's at war and it's not just the men who can fight."

"Lord, what's gotten into you?"

"They're not taking our winter's store of food, Billy King, nor our horses to ride down our Virginians with. Now crack those windows and hush. They're bringing Tempest and Sweetwater out of the stables. Master Ross is bound to take aim and shoot any minute."

The sound of the troopers' voices and the splash of the horses' hooves seemed loud to her once Billy had slowly opened each of the windows, keeping his head down and out of sight. She raised her head just enough to see what the Northerners were doing. They had three horses in tow, including Jupiter, and were moving away from the stables towards the barn.

Suppose they butcher our milk cows too? Malcolm, if you don't shoot soon they'll be too far from the house.

Sarah lifted her musket and poked it through an open window.

"What are you doing, Miss Sarah? Master Ross has to take the first shot, you said."

"Well, he hasn't, Billy King, and if we wait much longer we'll lose our chance."

He aimed her musket at the captain.

For a moment the feeling of Malcolm's lips on her neck and shoulder came back in a rush and she closed her eyes.

He was so sweet. He was so tender. But it was up to me to control things. We got carried away. Billy King is right – what's gotten into me? Six months ago I was eighteen and now it's as if I'm twenty-five or more. Malcolm and I aren't ready for marriage but we acted like two newlyweds in there. No more kisses. There can't be any more kisses.

She opened her eyes at the sound of Tommy and Billy King kneeling at their windows and aiming their muskets. She knew how good a shot both of them were. Billy glanced over at her.

"Right after you, Miss Sarah. If we don't shoot soon they'll be gone with our hogs and horses and probably our cows."

"Don't you both shoot the same man now."

"Uh-uh. Tommy's got the corporal leading out Tempest and I got the sergeant. I expect Master Ross has the captain lined up to rights."

"I can't count on Master Ross. I have the captain."

"Yes, Miss Sarah."

She lowered her cheek onto the musket stock and squinted with her left eye.

Too much has changed too fast. Papa should still be alive. And mama. My brothers should be here. I ought to still be walking around all day in a silk dress with plenty of hoops to my skirts. But now we have this war and these Yankees down here from Philadelphia and New York causing us grief. Why can't we just go our own way and have our own country? Why can't they leave us alone?

A shot cut through the wind and rain from the parlor windows. The captain staggered in his saddle. Sarah squeezed her trigger an instant later and the captain lurched to his left, fumbled for the reins of his horse, and toppled to the ground.

Tommy and Billy King fired at the same time. The sergeant slapped a hand to his shoulder. The corporal flew off his horse as if the wind had picked him up and hurled him.

Sarah did not even think. She picked up the musket leaning on the wall beside her, cocked back the hammer, aimed, and fired. The blast of Tommy's second musket was right after hers. Billy waited as a trooper began to charge the house, hollering, and shot him out of the saddle. The other troopers milled about in confusion, yanking out their revolvers and blazing away at the house. The windows in the kitchen shattered and Sarah went down to the floor as splinters of glass spun across the room.

"Oh!"

Tommy was slammed back into the kitchen table as bullets struck his left arm. Sarah saw blood spray onto the floor and chairs. She crawled to him as more bullets smacked into the walls or rang off pots sitting on the stove. Billy fired his third shot and ducked as what was left of the windows blew apart from revolver and carbine fire. Sarah reached Tommy and grasped one of his hands.

"I'm sorry, Miss Sarah."

"You have nothing to be sorry about, Tommy. You are very brave. I am going to bandage you and stop the bleeding. We'll get the bullets out later."

"But the soldiers – "

"Billy and Master Ross can handle them. You put two Yankees down. I saw that. Between the four of us half their men are out of the fight."

"There's still a powerful lot of bullets bouncing off the walls of this kitchen."

"Pistols have lots of shots to spare. But they're not hitting much."

He grinned, blood on his teeth. "Just me."

"Luck. Dumb Yankee luck. And they've pretty much used it up."

A shot ricocheted from the sink to the table to a chair by Sarah's head.

She squeezed Tommy's hand and smiled. "See? A clean miss."

"Yes, Miss Sarah, clean as a whistle."

She tore at the hem of her green dress.

"Just lay back, Tommy. Let me get these bandages on your arm."

"I hate to see you ruining your pretty green dress."

"I've got lots of pretty green dresses but my family has only ever had one Tommy."

Billy King fired.

"They're running, Miss Sarah!" he shouted. "They're a-running!"

"What about our horses?"

"They're loose. We'll catch 'em."

"And the smoked hogs?"

"They dropped most of them in the mud."

"Any sign of Master Ross?"

"No, Miss."

Malcolm burst into the kitchen, musket in his hands.

"Are you all right, Sarah?" he demanded. "Are you bleeding?"

"Get you head down!" she snapped. "It's not my blood!"

"They're gone. Headed back west into the valley."

"They could slip back and surprise us."

"They're not going to slip back. There are five of them on the ground."

It had all happened so fast it had been like her father training her to shoot as many tin plates as she could in three minutes. Now an image shot into her mind of a young face upturned and covered in rain. Malcolm saw her face go as white as bone as she tied off a second bandage on Tommy's arm.

"Are any of them wounded?" she asked.

"No."

"We need to go to them if they're wounded."

"None of them are wounded."

She kept her head down and worked at getting a third bandage in place.

Malcolm nodded to Billy King. "Reload your musket and put a cap on the nipple and come with me."

"Yes, sir."

"Where are you going?" Sarah's face was even whiter than it had been a moment before.

"To get the horses."

"Please be careful. I don't want any more killing."

"Neither do I."

Tommy's eyes were closed and his body was trembling.

"I'm going to get you a blanket," she told him.

"Yes, Miss Sarah." His eyes remained closed.

"The worst is over. The troopers are gone. You'll be all right."

"Yes, Miss Sarah."

She stood up slowly. Cold wind and rain blew through the kitchen from the broken windows.

She saw three bodies in blue uniforms sprawled in different positions on the grass.

Her hand went to her mouth.

It was red with Tommy's blood.

She ran from the room and bent over in the hallway. She was certain she would be sick but after a minute the feeling passed.

I must get a blanket for Tommy. Two blankets. And some hot coffee. As soon as Malcolm returns I will have him moved to a room that's warm. There's no time to act like a ten year old girl. There's no time to lose control.

She brought two woolen blankets from a closet and returned to the kitchen. Tommy tried to smile as she put them over him.

"I'm getting you some coffee, Tommy. Good hot coffee with plenty of sugar. All right?"

A chill went through her as the wind gusted over her wet dress. She stirred the embers in the wood stove to life and put water on to boil.

"I'll be right back."

Sarah raced from the kitchen and up the stairs to her room where she peeled off her dress and threw on another. Taking a heavy red shawl from a hook she wrapped it around her shoulders. Tommy was still breathing quietly when she returned. She quickly made a pot of coffee and poured him a mug, heaping sugar into it. Kneeling beside him she lifted his head and urged him to sip it while rain gusted over them.

"As soon as Master Ross is back we're moving you to a room with windows that still have glass in them."

"I'm all right," he mumbled. "Just get me to my room in the slave quarters."

"It's too far away. I won't have you getting more wet and chilled than you already are."

Malcolm stepped into the kitchen covered in mud.

She stared at him. "What happened to you? It looks like a team of horses dragged you through all the chuckholes in Virginia."

"That's pretty much it."

"Where are the horses?"

"Back in the stables."

"The hogs?"

"We picked up half a dozen of the carcasses."

"Where's Billy King?"

"Rubbing down your two. I fixed up Jupiter. He'll be along." He squatted by the door, musket in his hands. "How is he?"

"Holding his own."

"We'll likely have to take it off."

"We won't have it to take it off."

Malcolm smiled through the grime on his face. "You're quite the tiger now, aren't you? Mistress of Seven Oaks, Confederate sharpshooter, nurse and surgeon and all around Southern lady rolled into one hot temper."

"I don't have a hot temper. I don't have any temper at all." She stood up and placed the coffee cup on the table. "Help me get him to the library. I want him out of this draft."

"I'll board the windows up."

"I'm not going to wait till you board the windows up."

"Billy will be here in a minute or two."

"We don't need Billy King." She bent over and took Tommy's boots in her hands. "Are you going to help? Or shall I do it myself?"

"You can't lift him."

"I can lift him. I'm not from Richmond and I don't twirl parasols. The Blue Ridge Mountains are just over my shoulder and I grew up swimming in the Shenandoah River with my brothers. So am I on my own or are you going to get to your feet?"

Malcolm grunted and stood up, knees cracking. "They should have named you Stonewall. Not your uncle."

"You called me firebrand, didn't you? Isn't that good enough?"

"It goes with the red in your hair, yes."

"My hair is auburn with a dash of brown."

"I won't argue with you over it." He leaned his musket against a wall pitted with bullet holes and came over to put his hands under Tommy's shoulders and head. "Are you sure about this?"

"Will you please do your part so we can get on our way?"

They carried him to the library where Sarah wanted him laid out on the sofa.

"The blood will ruin your furniture."

"Like it's ruining my dress?"

"I didn't say that."

"Dresses and furniture can be replaced. Tommy has been with us since he was four." She ran a hand over Tommy's brow. "Is that better?"

"Yes, Miss," he whispered.

"I'll fetch you some more blankets." She glanced at Malcolm. "Where are you going?"

"To dig a grave for the men. I don't want foxes or coyotes or what not getting at them in the dark."

"Off behind the stables please. I will be out to help you in a few minutes."

"You are not going to help me dig Yankee graves in this storm."

"Of course I am. And Billy King will help too."

"Sarah – "

She was bringing blankets from a cupboard near a bookshelf.

"I'll get a fire started and then I'll be out. The digging will go much faster with three. Don't argue with the mistress of the plantation, Malcolm Beckett Ross."

Malcolm stared at her. "Who lit a fire under you today?"

"I expect the wood and tinder have been in place for years. It just needed a spark to get it going."

He went out the door. "Maybe Billy King and I'll be finished before you find us."

"I doubt it. And don't think of hiding away in the bushes somewhere. I'll spot you no matter where you go."

"You think so?"

"I do." Her brown eyes softened. "Malcolm. Bury them in a sweet place. They're some sister's brothers. I want them to have a Christian burial."

He nodded.

It took her longer than she thought to get a good blaze going in the stove. Then she made sure Tommy was as comfortable as she could make him before heading out the door. The wind caught her hair and blew it about her head and the rain felt like ice pellets against her face.

I must look like a wagon wreck. I don't care. I guess the tomboy really has come back to take up residence.

She followed tracks that showed where bodies had been dragged through the grass and mud to a spot fifty yards behind the stables. There was a horseshoe of young oaks and a shallow pit about three feet deep Malcolm and Billy King were still working on, piling the dirt and mud at the rim. The white faces of the Union troopers were all turned to the sky and storm. One looked no older than a boy of sixteen and his cheeks were covered in freckles. Sarah looked down at the rivers of rain between the toes of her boots and took several deep breaths.

"Is there another shovel?" she asked without raising her head.

"No, Miss," grunted Billy as he heaved out another load of dirt.

"We're almost done." Malcolm's shovel hit stone and she watched him wrestle with it out of the corner of her eye. "No need for you to climb in here."

She brought up her head. "Why don't they leave us alone?"

"Why, they consider us traitors, Sarah Nunley."

"There's a lot of land, a lot of room east to west. We can have two countries. There's another one on top of us, isn't there? Canada? So why can't there be three altogether?"

"Lincoln thinks we need to be one nation. The North agrees with him."

"These boys were our countrymen a year ago."

"I know that, Sarah."

"We need to say prayers over them."

"Well, you do that once we're ready."

It did not take much longer. Malcolm glanced at Billy King and nodded and they thrust their shovels into the mounds of earth. One after another they placed the bodies in blue uniforms in the grave, Malcolm taking the shoulders and head of each trooper, Billy the feet. They did not remove the troopers' boots or swords but Malcolm put aside four revolvers and two carbines.

"Here." Sarah took off her red shawl and handed it to Malcolm. "Put it over the face of the boy."

"He doesn't feel the storm anymore, Sarah."

"Put it over him, please."

Malcolm draped it carefully over the boy's chest and head. The rain soon shaped it to the trooper's face.

"If you want to pray now's the time to do it." Malcolm remained in the grave with Billy King. "Or would you rather I said the words?"

"I'm quite capable of handling it, Malcolm Beckett Ross. After the last two weeks I don't think there's anything that would make me flinch."

She bowed her head and the men did the same.

"Bless their souls, oh Lord our God, these young men so far from home, too far from home. The less of this I have to see the more gratitude I will express towards you. I long for this conflict to be over. I wish it would be finished by Christmas. Take care of my uncle and his men. Take care of the families and loved ones of the soldiers resting here. May they sleep in peace on this plantation a long, long time. A plantation in a free country. God have mercy on us all. Amen."

"Amen," said Malcolm and Billy King together.

They began to fill the grave, eventually climbing out and heaving shovelfuls of mud and earth onto the bodies. When they were done they walked past Sarah to the barn.

"Aren't you going to place a cross or a marker?" asked Sarah as they went by.

"The oaks are their marker," replied Malcolm.

She remained by the small hill of dirt until they came back.

"How are the cows?" Rain was pouring over her hair and face. "I'm afraid I forgot about them."

"Your slaves did their jobs. The barn is clean and there's fresh straw down. The cows have been milked."

"I guess we should head in then."

"If you're finished here, yes."

Billy King picked up the carbines and revolvers. He walked behind Malcolm and Sarah. Malcolm had his musket and Billy King's. The storm cut into their backs with its sharp wind and hard rain. No one spoke until they reached the mansion.

Sarah stopped and looked up at the white pillars and white verandah. "If we had to – if we could not get the bullets out – "

"I would amputate," Malcolm responded. "We have plenty of time to do that and save his life."

"Are you sure?"

"A lot of men had limbs amputated at Manassas. Most of them had to wait a few hours. They made out fine."

She managed a smile. "Thank you, Malcolm."

"It's nice to see one of those again."

"Heaven knows there's been few reasons to offer you one over the past couple of hours."

"I'm aware of that."

Billy King shouted: "Riders!"

Malcolm scarcely had time to react. He threw a musket to Billy and was lifting his to take aim when a dozen cavalrymen galloped around the corner of the mansion. Their horses were slick with mud and their uniforms spattered from boots to collars. Malcolm expected to see blue jackets and pants and for a split second that is what his eyes told him he saw.

"Lower your gun, Master Ross!" blurted Billy King. "They's our men."

The dozen riders were joined by two dozen more. They ringed Malcolm, pistols drawn. He dropped the musket down to his side.

"What is it, sergeant?" asked an officer trotting up on his bay. "Have you got one of those cussed Yankee raiders from Henderson's troop?"

"No, sir," replied the sergeant, his pistol pointed at Malcolm's heart. "I regret I have no Yankee. Though I've netted something just as good."

"What's that?"

"A deserter." He kept his revolver steady. "Isn't this the one they described to us, major?"

The major walked his horse through the cavalrymen and took a good look. "Are you Corporal Malcolm Beckett Ross?"

"Yes, sir," Malcolm responded.

The major nodded and turned to the sergeant. "Take him over to those oak trees yonder and hang him."

Firebrand

September, 1861, Seven Oaks

The sergeant nudged his horse forward and loosened a coil of rope from his saddle.

"You can't hang him!" Sarah grabbed Malcolm's hand. "General Jackson sent him down here!"

"I have no information on that," responded the captain.

"He sent letters requesting leave to stay longer at the plantation in order to assist me."

"I have no information on that either. He is on a list of deserters, plain and simple."

"He just helped fight off Yankee cavalry."

"Henderson's devils? Can you prove that?"

"We just buried them. Billy King can show you the grave."

The captain wiped the rain out of his eyes with a gauntleted hand. "Take a look, sergeant. Corporal Jennings, accompany the sergeant and the slave."

Billy King led the two mounted troopers into the trees.

The captain looked at Malcolm as he sat on his horse. "Even if what she says is true it doesn't mean I won't have you thrown in prison."

Malcolm stood at attention. "You may think the handsomeness of this woman explains it all to you, captain. But I was ordered to bring news of her father's death at Manassas to her. I was ordered to remain with her until she was settled into her role as mistress of the plantation. And I did my duty for Virginia and this woman of Virginia."

"No doubt."

Sarah's face flared red despite the cold rain. "What do you mean by that, captain? You'll look the proper fool if General Jackson shows up at Seven Oaks with you sitting there in the saddle interrogating us."

"Why would he show up here, ma'am?"

"I am his niece. We have entertained him here on several occasions."

"And can you prove that as well?"

Her eyes glittered with a sharp darkness. "Are you a Virginian, captain?"

"As it happens I am from Alabama."

"That explains a great deal."

The sergeant rode back from the woods. "Yankee troopers, sir. Pushed back just enough mud to get a look at their uniforms."

"Henderson's unit?"

"Yes, sir."

The captain stared at Malcolm. "Did you kill them?"

"Yes, sir."

He kept his eyes fixed on Malcolm. Then he made up his mind. "You fought for our country. We'll spare your neck. But we'll have you join our pursuit of the scoundrels. Get your gear together. Do you have your horse?"

"The Yankees tried to steal him but we got him back."

"Did you do all the shooting, Corporal Ross?"

"The slaves and Miss Nunley fought as well. Take a look at the kitchen windows, sir."

All eyes went to the house. Bullet holes peppered its walls especially at the kitchen. The windows were all blown out.

"No one hurt?" asked the captain.

"One of my best slaves is badly wounded," Sarah said. "I fear we may need to perform an amputation."

The captain wiped the rain out of his eyes again.

"Do you have anyone among your troopers who can do that for me, sir?" she asked.

He shook his head. "We have no time. I must get on those Yankees' backs. Ross, you have two minutes."

Malcolm strode to the stables.

"I honestly could use your help, sir," Sarah insisted. "He is of great value to us. He has served our family since he was a boy."

"I understand the importance of a good slave, believe me. But my orders are to pursue the Yankee raiders. I've already lost time here I couldn't afford."

Malcolm brought Jupiter out into the rain. "My hat is inside the house. And a few other items."

"Fetch them, man."

Malcolm returned in less than a minute, his gray cap on his head. He placed a boot in the stirrup and swung himself into the saddle.

"Make a tight tourniquet above the cut," he said to Sarah. "When you're done you must cauterize the stump to stop infection and bleeding."

"Malcolm, I can't possibly do that."

"You can. You've fought and now you can heal. There's no one else." His eyes were gray and blue and steady. "I think Sarah Felicity Nunley can do just about anything."

He turned his horse and rode off with the Confederate cavalry.

Sarah stood in the rain a moment. Then she narrowed her eyes and went inside, walking straight to her father's study. She removed a case of surgical tools from the top of the closet. Billy King held Tommy down while she cut with the saw. Tommy bit down on a hard piece of leather. As soon as she finished she brought a poker out of the fireplace that glowed white and red and applied it to Tommy's bleeding stump. His eyes rolled back and he passed out. Sarah ignored the stink of burnt skin and blood and continued to press the poker home, moving quickly from one spot to another. Once the wound was completely sealed she set the poker aside and put a bottle of brandy by Tommy's head. It had been in the surgical case.

"Stay with him," she ordered Billy King. "As soon as he wakes up make him drink it. We have to dull the pain."

"Yes, Miss Sarah."

"I don't care how much you give him. And untie the tourniquet."

"Yes, Miss Sarah."

"I'll ask Harriet and Letta to clean up the saw and bury the arm."

She left the room and went back outside, turning her face up to the storm. Tears and rainwater mixed. She stood like that for a long time.

December, 1861

"Troops coming on horseback, Miss Sarah! Virginians!"

Sarah came out onto the porch as Billy King called out.

"Ma'am." A rider reined in his horse and swept his wide-brimmed hat off his head. "Major General Jackson's compliments and he'd like to dine with you. Can you accommodate the general and a few of his officers?"

Sarah craned her neck. "Where are these officers and the general?"

"They'll be along directly."

"Why, that's wonderful. Of course we shall welcome him to our table. It so happens we have a ham roasting and it's a large one."

"I'm glad to hear it, ma'am."

"Now tell me – when did General Jackson become a major general?"

"About October 7th. It's been in all the newspapers, ma'am."

There was a thudding of hooves on the wet soil and a dozen riders came around the side of the house at a fast trot.

"Uncle!" Sarah lifted the hem of her dress and hurried down the steps. "They tell me you're a major general!"

"Praise God, my dear, praise God." He climbed down from his horse and put his arms around her. "I guess there's something left in this old warhorse yet." He held her at arm's length. "You look wonderful. All grown up."

"I had no choice."

The smile left his face. "No. You were called to a harder task. Have your slaves been obedient?"

"Yes, sir."

"Lieutenant Becket Ross tells me one was gravely wounded when Yankee raiders struck the plantation."

"He's fine, uncle, he's doing very well. *Lieutenant Becket Ross*?"

"Promoted for courage under fire when he helped apprehend the Yankee raiders. Personal recommendation by Captain Burns. Of course he fought the raiders here at Seven Oaks as well."

"Yes, sir."

"As did you." Jackson frowned. "Not something I want my niece doing more than once. Or any lady of Virginia."

"There wasn't a great deal of choice."

He gave her another hug. "You acquitted yourself well. We'll speak no more of it."

"So who has been offering you all this information about me?"

"The lieutenant himself, who else? He calls you the Firebrand."

"Firebrand?" Sarah could feel a flush moving up from her neck and over her face. "What sort of name is that for a young woman?"

Her uncle barked a laugh. "It suits a cavalry charger more than it does a belle like my niece, I'll grant you that. But he claims you've earned it."

"And where is this gentleman?"

"He's part of the rearguard. Are you able to handle a half dozen of us?"

"Of course, uncle. But what about the other men?"

"They have their field rations," he rumbled.

Sarah made a face. "That won't do. I will have Letta prepare a place for them in the parlor."

"Very well." Jackson smiled into his beard.

"Excuse me and I will see to the arrangements."

A cluster of officers rode up.

"Ah!" boomed Sarah's uncle. "I want to introduce you to my cavalry commander, Brigadier General James Ewell Brown Stuart, before you run off!" He said to her in a low voice, "Richmond sent him to me as an infantryman but I saw a cavalier in his eyes from the moment he arrived at my command."

The heavily bearded cavalry commander doffed his hat. "You must be the niece I hear so much about."

"How do you do, General? You have quite a name. It stretches from here to the Potomac."

All the men laughed, including her uncle.

"Mother was fond of names and couldn't decide so she dumped the whole hopper on me." He smiled. "Please call me Jeb."

"Jeb?"

"Yes, Miss Sarah. You're not one of my troopers so you needn't call me General. And you're not one of my enemies so I won't make you spell out the alphabet every time you address me. Jeb is made up of my initials. Fortunately they form a pronounceable name and one that is swift on the tongue."

"Suitable for a hard charging cavalry officer." Jackson's blue eyes gleamed. "Like Firebrand."

The blood went to Sarah's cheeks instantly. "The nickname seems to amuse you."

"It's entirely *apropos*. I should have thought of it myself."

"So has it gone the rounds of the whole Confederate army?"

"Whoever will give your beau a minute of their time hears about the name, I'm sure."

More blood darkened her face. "Uncle, he is not my beau. Has he been saying that as well?"

"Not in my hearing. But you can ask him yourself. Here is the newly minted lieutenant."

Malcolm came riding through the trees with two other men.

Sarah had been ready to give him her death look.

But she saw a young man who looked half a foot taller, with blacker hair, bluer eyes, and skin colored by wind and weather. He was wearing tall black cavalry boots and a wide-brimmed hat with one side turned up and had a saber buckled to his waist. She could see new strength in his arms and in his legs and when their eyes met, and he smiled at her, she felt a sudden heat burst in her head and blaze down through her body.

"Malcolm," she whispered.

He jumped down from his horse and saluted Jackson. "All's well, sir."

Jackson returned the salute.

Malcolm turned to Stuart and saluted again. "Back trail is clear, General, but I've posted two sentries."

"Good work."

Malcolm walked towards Sarah. For a moment she thought he was going to salute again but he tugged the gauntlet off his right hand and took her hand in his.

"I'm relieved to see you looking so well," he said. "I had no idea how you were doing. You didn't respond to any of my letters."

Along with the heat in her head and body, the touch of his hand made her feel even less like herself. "Letters? I didn't get any letters, lieutenant."

"I'm Malcolm to you, Sarah Nunley."

"Yes. Of course you are."

"No letters reached you at all? I sent seven."

"Seven? Seven what?"

"Seven letters."

Sarah shook her head and put her hand to her eyes for a moment. "Excuse me. What are we talking about?"

"Are you all right?"

Her head snapped up. "What? All right? Of course I'm all right. I'm perfectly fine." She shook his hand. "Welcome to Seven Oaks, lieutenant." She looked at her uncle and General Stuart. "I will go and get dinner arranged. How long will you be staying at Seven Oaks?"

"Several hours. My headquarters is located at Winchester," replied Jackson. "I'm in charge of military operations in the Shenandoah Valley."

"Winchester? But that's wonderful. That's less than a two hour ride."

"It is. So I hope to visit my niece on more than one occasion."

"Oh, I'd love that." She smiled at Stuart. "And you will bring your friends?"

"With your permission," rumbled Jackson.

"I can't think of anything more pleasant. It has been so lonely here, uncle."

He nodded. "I thought that might be the case. Praise the Lord, he has placed me very near to you."

She hugged him and kissed him on the cheek. "I'm so grateful. Let me run inside and get everything prepared. Please come to the dining room with your officers. And the enlisted men with you are warmly invited to the front parlor where they will be served." She squeezed her uncle's arm. "No need to remove boots and spurs."

"Nonsense. They'll track mud all over your carpet."

"I don't care. It's the least I can do for the soldiers of our country."

She turned to go and then stopped and glanced back at Malcolm. "I'm glad you accompanied Generals Jackson and Stuart, sir. I owe you a debt for how you helped me out in September and the manner in which you defended this plantation."

"No debt is owed me. You are a lady of Virginia and one of its brightest stars. It was my duty. And an honor."

Sarah saw her uncle's eyes gleam with approval at Malcolm's words.

She didn't want to say anything else but could not bite her tongue. "Lieutenant Malcolm Becket Ross, you drive a woman to distraction. You are the most gallant man I know. And you are dressed like the most gallant man I know. I had just collected my thoughts before you stood them on their heads again."

"I apologize if I – "

She waved her hand. "Please join your commanding officers inside. After you have seen your men to the front parlor with their boots on."

He smiled. "Is that an order?"

She smiled back. "Yes, it is. You are at my headquarters now and all of you are under my command. See to your horses and men. And I will make sure something is set aside for your sentries."

Malcolm bowed again with a broad sweep of his hat. "Yes, sir, Miss Sarah Felicity Nunley. It's a pleasure to do my duty for Old Virginia."

It took another hour to get the meal ready in quantities Sarah felt would be sufficient. Until then Harriet and Tommy, who worked as quickly with one arm as he had with two, served the officers and men coffee and biscuits. Once dinner was served prayers of thanks were offered up in both the parlor and the kitchen for God's blessing and the success of Confederate arms. Then the soldiers went at the ham and sweet potatoes and peas with great enthusiasm.

"How are you situated in Winchester?" Sarah asked her uncle as they ate. "Not in some rude log structure they have thrown up, surely."

"By no means. It is a pleasant house that was offered to me by a most gracious citizen. It is small, to be sure, but it has two stories and provides more than enough room for myself and my staff."

"And is Lieutenant Ross attached to your staff?"

Jackson chewed on a slice of ham and shook his head. "He is not," he said after he had swallowed. "Since his exploits with Captain Burns' troopers in bringing the Yankee raiders to bay I've attached him to General Stuart's command."

"How does that suit you, General Stuart?"

Stuart smiled. "Jeb, please, Miss Sarah. Why, it suits me fine. He's a good horseman and has a keen mind and a quick eye. Soon enough he'll be after my job."

Jackson pointed at Stuart with his spoon. "And then you'll be after mine."

The men at the table roared and Sarah caught Malcolm's eye for a moment. She put as much warmth as she could into her look. To her surprise, she saw a brief flash of crimson pass over his features.

Well, well, you really do feel something for me, Malcolm Becket Ross. It hasn't been out of sight, out of mind after all. I suspect you really did send seven letters that are lost and I believe you truly have been wandering about telling the soldiers of the Confederate army that I am a firebrand.

"How have you been faring, Miss Sarah?" asked Stuart. "You have lost both your father and your mother since the start of this war. My condolences."

"Thank you . . . Jeb. I think I have things in hand now. My household servants and my field hands have done everything I've asked of them and more. The plantation is getting along as well as it ever has. How about you, sir? Where is your home?"

"Well, I was raised on a plantation much like this in Patrick County, near the North Carolina border. My wife and I lived in Fort Riley, Kansas, where I served in the army, until our great nation was born and I resigned to take up my post with the Confederacy. Our home is in Virginia now and I have two splendid children who will be raised in freedom."

Several of the officers clapped at his words.

"That's wonderful." Sarah turned to look at Jackson. "Uncle. I think you would like a bowl of fruit to dip into after your meal."

"I would. Do you have oranges or peaches?"

"Well, it is December, but I do have peaches preserved in jars. I shall ask Letta to bring some to the table. More to your liking, I have apples in barrels in the cellar and they are as crisp and juicy as the day they were picked."

"The apples sound like just the thing to round off this blessed repast."

Sarah pushed herself back from the table and stood up, flashing her eyes at Malcolm as she did so. "I will see to it."

"Sit down, my dear. Surely your servants can take care of that."

"The preserves they can. But I have a special barrel of the reddest apples that I have set to one side. It will be best if I tend to that and fill a bowl for the General and his men. Excuse me a minute."

She left the dining hall and went down the hall to the door that led to the cellar. Opening it, she stepped inside and left it ajar, taking a candle from her pocket, lighting it, and waiting. Finally she heard the rapid tread of boots and the door swung wide.

"Sarah?"

"Shh." She grabbed Malcolm's hand and pulled him inside, shutting the door firmly.

It was completely black except for the small candle flame that lit up both their faces.

"Did you really write me seven letters?" she asked.

"I wouldn't lie to you."

"What did you say in them?"

"I don't remember."

"Of course you remember. Tell me. Please."

She brought the candle close to his face so she could see him better.

"Why, I said – I said, why, that I missed you, that I hoped you were well and your slave was well, I asked if you had done the amputation, I asked if your slaves were behaving, how the harvest had – "

"Malcolm Becket Ross." Her voice was low. "You are driving me to distraction again. Tell me what you said from your heart."

"I said – I said that – " He stopped. "I wrote that I loved kissing you more than anything in the world. Better than food and drink. Better than air. Better than horses and sabers and the whole army and Confederate States of America."

"You didn't."

"Yes, I did."

She still had his hand. "Let's go down to the cellar."

"You'll get chilled."

"Not if you do your job."

Candle in front of her, still gripping his hand, she descended the stairs. At the bottom they stood on an earthen floor. The cellar smelled of carrots and potatoes and dirt. She tugged him towards the large barrels of apples.

"Hold this." She put the candle in his hand.

"Sarah – "

She put her arms around his neck. "Prove it."

"What?"

"Prove I'm better than armies and nations and food and the air you breathe."

The candle flame made her face like gold. Her eyebrows changed color, and her eyes, and her skin, and even her hair, tucked up on her head. With one arm he brought her against his chest. With his lips he covered her mouth. The kiss was so long and so gentle and so strong, all at the same time, that Sarah thought she was going to sink to the ground from the sheer pleasure of it.

"So are you going to buy a red-lined cape like your hero?" she whispered, when they broke apart for a moment.

"If I ever have the money."

"Perhaps I'll have one sent to you for a Christmas present."

"The mail doesn't work for us."

"Oh, this will work. I'll bring it in person."

"Sarah. You can't. What if the Yankees sent raiders into the valley again? You could get shot."

"They wouldn't harm a woman."

"Not on purpose but – "

"Tell me something else from the lost letters."

"I don't – "

"Please. Heaven knows when I'll see you again."

"I said I thought I might maybe be, you know."

"What?"

"Well, be feeling something for you."

"You thought you might be feeling something for me? Maybe?"

"I wrote it better than that, Sarah. I said I thought about you all the time, that I went over and over the moment we kissed and couldn't keep it out of my mind and didn't want to. I said you came to my dreams whether I was sleeping or awake. In the last letter I asked if I might not be in love with you. And that if I was in love with you, would that be all right or would you be angry?"

"Angry?"

She brought his head down and kissed him with everything she could bring to bear – her youth, her strength, her womanhood, her loneliness, her fear, her hope, and she would not stop, pressing him against a barrel of apples and putting the weight of her whole body behind her kiss.

They could hardly breathe when she finally pulled back.

"How's that for a firebrand?" she whispered, smiling.

"You're hotter than the mouth of a cannon."

"Would you like some more, lieutenant?"

"Yes, please. I'm fair starved for proper nourishment."

Her lips burned against his lips and her body burned against his body, all of it coming together to press him harder and harder against the staves of the barrel.

"Now uncle will be wondering about his apples," she said, taking her mouth away and running her finger over the contour of his lips.

"I wish he wouldn't," Malcolm replied.

She kissed his chin and cheek and ear. "The candle's almost gone."

"We don't need it."

She smiled as the flame flickered over her face. "What a perfect lover you have turned out to be. Who would have guessed it when we were children?"

"One of God's mysteries."

"It is one of God's mysteries."

"Shall we explore it further?"

She laughed. "You can always ask me to marry you. But don't do that today. I'll say no."

"Why would you say no?"

"It's too soon. Come to me again. Bring uncle and Jeb if you must. Win the war so we can put that behind us. Then ask me."

"I don't know when I'll get back to Seven Oaks."

"Neither do I. But whenever it is, I'll be ready for your question. Make sure you're ready too."

"I've prayed about it."

"I'm glad."

"I even went to the chaplain. I never used your name, of course."

"Thank you."

"Just called you a firebrand."

"No, you didn't."

"A firebrand smoking away in a corner of my heart."

She brushed her lips lightly over his. "Once it's all of your heart that's the time to ask me for my hand, Lieutenant Malcolm Becket Ross."

March - July, 1862

Never one to read the newspapers, Sarah had the Richmond papers delivered to her door from the beginning of the new year. Her uncle was defeated in a battle at Kernstown in the Shenandoah Valley in March – it caused her to pray harder for the birth struggles of her nation as well as the safety of her uncle and Malcolm and their men. Her prayers seemed to be rewarded by a string of victories for Stonewall Jackson at McDowell, Front Royal, Winchester, Cross Key and Port Republic. The papers sang his praises day in and day out – *With a handful of troops General Jackson has humbled Yankee forces three to four times the size of his own. He has struck so swiftly it is as if all his soldiers were mounted on horses. They are Jackson's foot cavalry and because of their speed and fighting spirit Lincoln has withdrawn all Union troops from the Shenandoah Valley. It is a great victory.*

But the same papers made it clear the fight was not going so well closer to Richmond and that was where General Stuart was located and Malcolm with him. Northern troops were pushing Confederate forces back on the capital. Due to the mud and the rain the Southern cavalry were hardly used at all which made Sarah feel an odd mixture of emotions – relief that Malcolm was out of harm's way but disappointment that her brave young man would not be permitted an opportunity to win the day for the Confederacy.

She began to make it her practice to pray for her nation when she woke up in the morning, immediately after lunch, and before bed each night. Harsh battles on the very outskirts of Richmond forced Confederate General Joseph E. Johnston out of command with a severe wound. He was replaced by General Robert E. Lee, a man Sarah had scarcely heard of, on June 1st. Nothing happened for weeks. Then news came to her doorstep that Stuart and the cavalry were on the move, probing the flank of the Union army, quickly followed by the announcement that her uncle had come to Richmond with his foot cavalry. Battles bloomed all over the Virginia Peninsula in late June, some won by General Lee and her uncle, others lost. Earlier in the month she had read newspaper reports criticizing Lee as the King of Spades for building up the defenses around Richmond but failing to go on the attack. Now she read reports criticizing her uncle for being late and ineffective at the battles of Gaines' Mill, Savage's Station, and White Oak Swamp. Tears cut down her cheeks.

"What do you expect?" she shouted out loud in the library, throwing her newspaper to the floor. "He is not a young man anymore and you make him do all your fighting for you in the Valley! Then you drag him to Richmond and want him to save the day for you there as well! How fortunate you are he hasn't drop dead from exhaustion!"

In the end the Union army withdrew and the threat to the Confederate capital ended, but Sarah still smarted from the blows rained on her uncle by the press. For more than two weeks she refused to open the papers that came to Seven Oaks until Malcolm's parents came by in their carriage to ask if she'd heard the news.

"Stuart's cavalry ran rings around the Union forces," Mr. Becket crowed. "Why, they circled the whole army and captured over a hundred soldiers and more than two hundred mules and horses as well as untold wagonloads of supplies. The citizens threw flower petals in front of Stuart and the boys when they returned to Richmond a few days ago. What a marvelous ending to a difficult spring and summer."

Mrs. Becket smiled and patted his arm. "You haven't mentioned the best news of all."

"Ah, of course. Malcolm is promoted to captain for capturing three platoons of Yankee infantry without losing a single man. Isn't that something?"

Sarah smiled. "Yes, it is."

"Do you ever hear from our Malcolm at all, Miss Sarah?" asked Mrs. Becket.

"No, ma'am."

"He is very busy, very busy, as you can imagine, but he does write us once a month religiously. Are you keeping well, my dear? Do you need a hand with anything here?"

"The plantation is doing splendidly, thank you, ma'am."

"Don't hesitate to send a slave over with any requests."

Again Sarah wrestled with mixed emotions – joy that Malcolm was safe and was now a captain, sadness that she had not received one letter from him since he had visited Seven Oaks in December, not even a thank you note for the red-lined cape she had sent. This lasted for several days until one morning a postal clerk drove up while she was taking fresh air on the porch.

"A warm July, Miss Sarah," he said as he climbed down from his carriage.

"It is, Mr. Buckley." She continued to fan herself.

He came up on the porch. "I have good news and bad news. The bad news is your mail has been sent to the wrong address since last fall. I apologize for this although it was not my doing. The good news is I have all that mail with me today." He produced a thick packet of letters. "That hero of yours must write in the saddle."

Sarah dropped her fan and jumped to her feet. "Those are mine?"

"They are." He put the bundle of envelopes wrapped in string in her hand. "Curiously, there is a woman in Richmond with your name who lives on a street called Oaks something or other and that is where the army sent your mail. The dear old lady, Mrs. Sarah Nunley, a widow living on her own, set every letter aside, realizing they were not for her, and never opened one of them. But she never informed anyone about the matter either. She died two weeks ago, may she rest in peace, and one of her daughters took the trouble to deliver these to the main post office in Richmond for proper delivery."

"My goodness, Mr. Buckley!"

"Some story, hm? Now it's like Christmas in July for you." He tipped his hat to her. "I reckon that young man sets great store by you."

"Thank you, Mr. Buckley. God bless you, sir."

She dropped back in her chair as he drove away and opened every envelope and read every letter. Malcolm's handwriting was scribbled over sheets of paper marked October and November and December of 1861 as well as through the first six months of 1862. There was a thank you for the cape that he wore constantly and which had prompted one of his men to tease him as *Little Jeb*. The letters after the December visit almost scorched her fingers – she was more beautiful than light, her kisses were hot sparks on his lips, holding her was like holding the moon and stars and all the comets, one look from her eyes sent lightning through his whole body. She put a hand to her mouth when she was only halfway through the stack.

"Oh, my heavens," she whispered.

I love you, he wrote before he joined Stuart's cavalry in their dash around the Union army. *If I die, remember I loved you. If I live, let me love you more than any man has loved any woman. If God lets me come to you again at Seven Oaks please bless me forever with a yes, a yes, a yes.*

August and September

My dear Sarah,
It has been a very busy series of campaigns what with the fighting in the Valley and along the Peninsula but, I thank God, he has blessed our endeavors and we have repelled the invaders. I hope you are in good health and that you have everything well in hand on the plantation.

I am dashing off this note for we are on the move again. You asked two questions. Your beau, who you say is not your beau, I have placed under General Stuart and you asked after the General's character and deportment. There is no finer officer or cavalryman than Jeb. He will not have anything to do with alcohol or tobacco, his language is clean, his love for God and Christ and Virginia pure and consistent. He is confident before God in his abilities and, much like myself, is more than eager to carry the fight to the enemy. He never entertains a black thought but is altogether optimistic about the outcome of any enterprise he sets his hand to. You may rest content that Captain Ross is well blessed to be an officer under General Stuart's command.

The second question and then I must go. You asked what I did with my slaves. Why, I set them free, Sarah, I set them free.
My love and prayers
Uncle Thomas
Psalm 23:5

"Are they all assembled, Billy King?"
"Yes, Miss Sarah."
"All the field hands? Jimmy Buck? Cleveland?"
"Yes, Miss Sarah."
She got up from her chair in the library, setting down the Richmond paper with its headline about a Confederate victory at Bull Run Creek, and went out onto the porch. Her household slaves

and field slaves were standing below in the August heat. There were just over a dozen and Billy King walked down the steps to join them.

"What I am about to say I have prayed about and thought about a good while," she began. "My neighbors may well differ from me in my opinions on this matter and may indeed oppose what I am about to do. That doesn't concern me. I only wish to live rightly in the eyes of the Lord. We have a new country. We have a New South. Virginia is freer than it has ever been since the American Revolution. Keeping all that in mind, a number of issues need to be addressed in our newly liberated nation and one of them is slavery. My uncle is done with it and so am I and so is Seven Oaks. Henceforth, from this day forward, you are free. Free as the birds. I will be discussing this with our local law officials so they understand that none of you are to be considered runaways if you wish to make your way to another county or state. You will be given documents to that effect signed by a local judge. I have nothing else to say. You may pack up and leave as soon as you wish. You are not bound to this plantation anymore. Indeed you are not bound to any plantation or to any man. You are God's children and all God's children must be free."

The slaves glanced at one another and began to whisper but no one shouted and only a few smiled.

Billy King stepped forward. "How are you going to work this plantation on your own, Miss Sarah?"

"I will advertise for hired hands, Billy King."

"Suppose some of us wished to stay on, Miss Sarah?"

"Why, if any of you would like to stay and work for me you are free to do so. You will be given room and board and an honest man's wage – the same wage I would give any white man."

Now there were smiles; now there was even some laughter.

Billy King glanced around him and nodded. "There may be a few who want to press on or head north. But most of us want to stick with you, Miss Sarah. We will take care of the tobacco and take care of the farm from dawn to dusk. And we will take care of you as well."

Sarah stood up straight and smiled. "I do not think I need taking care of, Billy King, I can do that well enough on my own. But I thank you for your desire to care for this plantation. And I am grateful to have so many of you choose to remain at Seven Oaks.

The word slave will no longer be tolerated here. None of you may use it nor may any of my guests. Henceforth you are household staff or field hands. Is that clear?"

Billy King grinned and tossed his hat in the air. "It sure is, Miss Sarah! Glory hallelujah! Free at last, free at last, thanks God Almighty, I'm free at last!"

"Yes, Billy King, thank God. Thank God for a new start for our new country. And a new start for all of you."

"I don't expect every Virginian will agree with y'all, Miss Sarah."

"I don't care if they do or not. I just care what God thinks. And what I think along with him."

Dear darling Sarah,
We have had some stiff fighting in Virginia and to the north. The clash at South Mountain in Maryland was hot work. I am still in one piece. Despite all my hours in the saddle I can't stop thinking of you. I wish you'd write a letter with the words in it I long to hear.
Malcolm

My sweet Malcolm
These letters take a long time to make their way back and forth. If you wish to hear certain words from me come in person. Only that will do. Alive and well and in person. May God guard you through this perilous campaign. I read about the fighting in Maryland several days ago. It was hard to finish the newspaper. The day at Sharpsburg sounds like a nightmare. I hold on firmly to the belief that you are all right.
My deepest prayers and deepest affection
Sarah Felicity

Darling Sarah
I have just come through the worst fighting I've been in. So many men and horses litter the battlefield at Sharpsburg it's best not to think about it. A comrade, Jim Page, was shot out of the saddle by cannon fire. He was riding right next to me. I have posted a note to his mother. I have no idea if my letters are getting through to her or to you. We are withdrawing from Maryland and are on our way back to Virginia. We cannot continue the campaign

against the Yankees without rest and reinforcements. Now I think they will be after us and unhappily the battleground will be the Old Dominion once again. Regardless of the bloodiness of this war my affection for you remains untarnished and undiminished. It probably shines brighter the more of war's grim visage I see. Love is the hope of our new nation. That is what we are fighting for – a free nation bountiful with love and peace.

My heart is in your hands
Malcolm

Dearest Malcolm
Where are you? If you are in Virginia again and you have even an hour of freedom you must come to me. All this fighting has been wretched to sit through and pray through. I snatch up newspapers in sheer agony of what I might find from one day to the next. Oh, please come to me, I can't bear to wait another day, another week, another month.

Longing for you
Your Sarah

"Riders, Miss Sarah! Virginians!"

"Oh!" Sarah dropped her Bible on her chair and ran from the parlor to the front porch.

Three young men in gray galloped up in front of the house. One of them jumped down.

"Malcolm! Oh, my Lord, thank you!"

She practically leaped down the steps and hurtled into his arms, knocking him back.

"I only have an hour," he said. "No more."

She gripped him as tightly as she could. "That's enough. My prayers are answered."

"My boys will grant us leave to disappear."

She pulled back from him a moment. "Your men are welcome here. Please rest and water your horses. My household staff will bring you food and drink. You can sit on the porch or go inside to the library, whichever you like. Billy King?"

"Yes, Miss Sarah," responded Billy King. "Let me take your horses, sirs."

"Why, thank'ee kindly," said one of the troopers as he dismounted.

Sarah took Malcolm by the hand and led him into the house and down the hall.

"Letta!" she called out. "There are Virginians to see to on the front porch!"

"Yes, Miss Sarah."

She tugged Malcolm out the back door and onto the path that ran through the woods. Once they were surrounded by bushes and ferns and trees, and could not be seen from the house, she spun around and locked him in her arms and covered his mouth with hers. She was determined to give him a kiss he would never forget and one she would never regret holding back on. Her fingers curled in his shining black hair and she kissed him harder and harder, pressing him back against a tree trunk just as she had pressed him back against a barrel of apples nine months before. She broke the kiss for a split second to whisper, *"I love you, sweetheart, I love you,"* before drawing his head back down to hers.

"You sure are warm and soft and sweet," he managed to get out between kisses.

"You bet I'm warm and soft and sweet. Now that I've said what I've wanted to say, do you have anything you'd like to say to me in return?"

"Yes, I do."

"Well, get on with it. We only have so much time."

"You sound like your uncle and Jeb Stuart both."

"I can't help it. I feel like I'm in the middle of a cavalry charge. You drop out of the sky and tell me that we have an hour. Now it's less than forty-five minutes, I'm sure."

"I'm equal to the task."

He went to one knee, sweeping off his hat with its broad brim and turned up side, and grasping her hand.

"Sarah Felicity Nunley," he said, "nothing could make me happier on God's green earth than if you were to become my bride."

She smiled and put her other hand over her mouth. "I can't believe this is happening."

"I've fought through a lot of Yankees to get here and I won't take no for an answer."

"No?"

"No."

"What are your intentions if you marry me?"

"To cherish you. Bring you cut flowers in vases. Kiss you morning, noon, and night. Draw your bathwater for you at just the right temperature. Saddle your horse and – "

"Yes."

He stopped. "Yes?"

"Yes."

"Just like that?"

"Just like that."

"But I have a lot more to say."

"Put it in a letter." She tugged him to his feet and nuzzled his handsome face with her lips. "We have so little time and I'd rather kiss than talk."

"But Sarah, I – "

"Shh, Captain Ross." She planted slow kiss after slow kiss on his mouth. "You had me at the moment you said you'd draw my bathwater for me at just the right temperature."

A Wedding In Virginia

December 17, 1862
My beautiful Sarah

You will have read about the fight at Fredericksburg. I have come through without a scratch. The Yankee attack, of course, has delayed our wedding plans. I cannot see our marriage taking place in the time remaining to us in 1862. But with the North back where they belong and licking their wounds I am hopeful you and I may become man and wife early in January. I am counting the days.
All my love,
Your Malcolm

January 3rd, 1863
My lovely Sarah,
A brand new year! I am hopeful before God it will be the best year of my life because, on the one hand, the year will see me married to the most beautiful woman in Virginia and, on the other hand, it will see the triumph of our armies and the full and complete independence of a Southern nation. I pray every day for both to come to pass. I am scribbling this off to wish you every blessing in the year ahead and to make sure you know you are in my thoughts morning, noon, and night and how delightful those thoughts are to me.
All my love,
Your Malcolm

January 22nd, 1863
Dearest Sarah,
Well, confound those Yankees and their General Burnside! Will they never leave well enough alone? Haven't they placed enough of their men in graves in Virginia? Perhaps the Richmond papers have told you of the Northerners' march into the Old Dominion? The roads and pathways are nothing but water and mud yet this Burnside fellow

seems determined to regain the honor lost him and his army at Fredericksburg. What it means for us is that I and the Army of Northern Virginia must remain at our post. There can be no wedding while the Yankees are up to their devilry and I am the most disappointed bridegroom in the South because of it. I am praying for a quick and ignominious end to their latest invasion and, to tell you the truth, one that does not result in as a great a shedding of blood as we saw at Fredericksburg. I was glad God blessed our army with a victory but, by the time it was over, I was heartily sick of the slaughter.

    I hope my next letter shall bring you happier news and the announcement that you will be free to go ahead and fix a date for the wedding.

    All my love,
    Your Malcolm

January 30th, 1863
My Sarah,
I thank God! A bloodless victory! I suppose some might not call it a victory since the two armies never met one another in the field, but the Yankees have turned back, and that is good enough for me. I imagine they are still scraping the mud off their boots and muskets and cannon. And Burnside is gone. Abraham Lincoln has placed Joseph Hooker in charge of the Army of the Potomac in his stead. It is my hope and prayer he is their last general for my sense of it is the war will be finished this summer and the North will stay on their side of the border forever after one or two more good lickings.

    I will write again very soon and I believe I shall have grand news for you.

    Missing you with all my heart,
    Malcolm

February 2nd, 1863
Lovely Sarah,
How swiftly can you prepare Seven Oaks for the wedding? The Yankees have finally dug themselves in for the winter and I have been granted leave to make my way to your plantation and take you as my lawfully wedded wife. Not only that, but your uncle will be accompanying me for he is determined to give you away. Good friends will be at his side – who they are may surprise you but I say nothing

more for the time being. We have the weekend of the 14*th* as a gift from the Army of Northern Virginia, General Robert E. Lee commanding. How does a wedding on a Saturday suit you?
Much love,
Malcolm

PRECIOUS MALCOLM
I HAVE NEVER SENT A TELEGRAM BEFORE SO I HOPE THIS REACHES MY SWEET MALCOLM DESPITE ALL THE SERIOUS MILITARY MEN WHO ARE STANDING BETWEEN YOU AND ME. I HAVE MADE PLANS FOR THE WEDDING TO TAKE PLACE AT OUR PLANTATION ON SATURDAY THE 14TH. I TRUST ALL WHO ACCOMPANY YOU SHALL FEEL FREE TO SPEND THE NIGHT FOR WE HAVE PLENTY OF BEDROOMS AND CLEAN BED LINEN. I CAN HARDLY WAIT TO BE YOUR BRIDE.
YOUR SARAH

BEAUTIFUL SARAH
ALL THE YANKESS IN THE ARMY OF THE POTOMAC COULD NOT KEEP ME AWAY. WE WILL ARRIVE ON FRIDAY THE 13TH AND THAT WILL BE GOOD LUCK FOR ME.
MALCOLM

February 5th
My dearest Sarah,
As I sit here and reminisce about your childhood, I am astonished to think you will be raising children of your own in a few years. How the Lord blesses and provides for us from one season to another. I am honored to give you to Captain Malcolm Beckett Ross and I know your parents would be delighted with your choice. He is brave, chivalrous, devoted to God and Virginia and his commanding officers and men. In addition, he is devoted to you, and this, taken with all the rest, pleases me greatly.
Generals Stuart and Lee shall accompany me to this sacred event. A good number of General Stuart's troopers will form an honor guard. I know your bridegroom wished the attendance of such fine and revered commanding officers to remain a secret until next Friday, but in truth I did not wish you to be caught unawares in any way, knowing how my own wife is greatly discomfited when such surprises

occur. The entire party will be staying the night at Seven Oaks if that is not too much trouble. I believe you still have all your household servants, do you not, for you told me all of them had chosen to remain at Seven Oaks? If our extended presence should prove an inconvenience I know you will inform me.

My deepest affection and my prayers,
Uncle Thomas
Proverbs 5:18

GENERAL THOMAS JONATHAN JACKSON
I RECEIVED YOUR LETTER ON THE NINTH. SO HERE I AM SENDING A TELEGRAM FOR THE SECOND TIME IN MY LIFE. BUT I DID NOT WISH YOU TO SET OUT NOT KNOWING HOW I FELT ABOUT OVERNIGHT GUESTS. THERE IS NOTHING I SHOULD LIKE BETTER. MALCOLM AND I SHALL NOT EMBARK ON OUR THREE DAY HONEYMOON UNTIL MONDAY. ALL THOSE FAMOUS MEN UNDER THE NUNLEY ROOF – MOMMA WOULD BE FRANTIC. HOWEVER I AM CALM AS THE WATERS OF A SWAN POND. MY GIRLS DO ALMOST EVERYTHING. AND WHAT THEY DON'T DO MY BOYS DO.
SARAH

February 10th, 1863
Dearest Sarah,
I have a courier who swears he can get this to the nearest and best postmaster so that the letter is in your hands before I arrive. For how can I marry you on the 14th without offering you a paper valentine from a secret admirer first? The truth is I never thought to send you a valentine with the war on. But now that I feel we are close to winning it I feel more lighthearted about the matter. A woman as lovely as you must have a valentine from a secret admirer at least once in her life. I was able to purchase this from one of my men whose sister sent him a bushel of paper valentines – I take it she felt he needed to do something about his love life or lack of it. His blessing became my boon.

I hope you like the valentine. If you do you may tell me in an appropriate manner once we see each other face to face.

My unending love and devotion,
Malcolm

February 13th, 1863, Seven Oaks
"Are they all polished?"

"Miss Sarah, they are polished to a shine. They are polished to rival the sun and stars. Everything is. Every candlestick holder, every silver fork, spoon, and knife, every tray, every window, why even the rugs and carpets and curtains have been dusted and polished both."

Sarah laughed. "Well, that should impress a fine old gentleman like General Lee. I'm sure he's never seen curtains dusted to a shine."

"The beds are made and the rooms aired. The touch of rain gives them all a wonderful fragrance."

"And the lamps – "

"The lamps all have fresh wick in them and plenty of oil and every candle in the house is new. We only have a few older candlesticks in the main rooms to use tonight."

"What about the meals? It's not just the generals I'm worried about but all the other men."

"Well, stop worrying and fretting, Miss Sarah; Letta and I have that just where we want it, and there'll be plenty of fixings for everyone."

"You know I had hoped we could hold a ball after the wedding ceremony."

"Haven't you told us that a thousand times? The men with their instruments will be here in good time come Saturday evening and they'll begin with a round of *Dixie,* Mr. Samuels told me, before moving on to General Lee's Grand March and then some fine Southern waltzin' music."

"We have so many guests, Harriet – "

"Look, now." Harriet rested her hands on her hips, smiling. "You just fix your mind on getting married. Did you like that there gown from Missus Hannicott in Richmond?"

"I did."

"And you tried it on?"

"Not above a hundred times. The new girl, Ellie, she had to bring it in in a few places, but, my, she has fingers as swift and neat as swallows – "

"She is a wonder, Miss Sarah."

" – and now I feel like I'm living in some sort of enchantment and waiting for my prince."

"Oh, he's coming Miss Sarah, and once he arrives he'll be flesh and bone like you and me, he won't be no enchantment or spell."

"Why, he's here already." Letta poked her head into the parlor with a smile. "Billy King just got a mighty interesting letter addressed to you in the morning mail, Miss Sarah."

Sarah straightened in her chair. "Where is it?"

"He'll bring it along."

"Bring it along? Where on earth is he going first?"

"For a silver platter." Billy King walked into the parlor. A red envelope lay on a shiny tray. "Here you are, Miss Sarah. Compliments of the Army of Northern Virginia."

"I've never seen a red envelope before." Sarah snatched it from the tray and tore it open. "My goodness. I've never had a valentine before either."

"That's real lace around the edges." Letta was craning her neck from the doorway.

"And nice red ribbon too." Harriet nodded her head. "This is going to be a special wedding. I feel it in my bones. So many special things have happened already."

Sarah read the letter that accompanied the valentine and opened the valentine up, quickly going over what Malcolm had written inside, her lips moving. A flush spread from her neck and throat and onto her cheeks and forehead.

"I don't guess we're gonna hear what Master Ross wrote you, are we, Miss Sarah?" asked Harriet.

Sarah closed the valentine and slipped it back into the envelope with a smile. "The wedding is public. Not his love poems. Our guests will be here by evening. Let's return to our preparations."

"I think everything is just about done, Miss Sarah."

"Well, I'm afraid I have another idea so far as decorating the ballroom goes, Harriet."

Harriet looked at the envelope in Sarah's hand. "You don't mean valentines?"

Sarah got to her feet. "And I shall help."

"Mm-hm. That's a good idea. I just hope we have the paint we need to turn white paper red."

"Come with me to my room." Sarah headed out of the parlor and up the staircase. "My childhood watercolor sets are still in excellent condition. I shall paint and you shall cut. Or the other way around."

Harriet came up the staircase behind Sarah. "I can do both. You need to rest."

"I need to do something. I am going to go wild if I don't keep busy, absolutely wild."

"In that case I'd best have the scissors, Miss Sarah, and you ought to stick to the brush."

Sarah laughed. "Agreed."

A long lane of lanterns hanging from poles had been set up and lit by Jimmy Buck and Cleveland. It extended for a quarter mile and as the first troopers trotted their horses towards the mansion they rode between them with surprise on their faces. Coaches that had been hired and were waiting at the railroad station rolled over the wet February track behind the cavalrymen. Sarah was at the foot of the steps to the porch and front doors in a silk gown of scarlet. She welcomed General Lee and his wife as they exited the first coach, Billy King opening the coach doors for them.

"I am honored to have you at Seven Oaks, General, and I'm so pleased you have brought your wife up from Richmond."

The General bent to kiss her white-gloved hand. "The honor is mine. General Jackson has often mentioned his beautiful niece and it is a blessing to put away the weapons of war for a few hours and see her wed to a Virginia man. The Lord bless you, my dear."

"Thank you, sir. Mrs. Lee, how grateful I am you were able to accompany your husband."

Mrs. Lee patted Sarah's cheek. "My husband wants to set warfare aside for a day. I love Richmond, but I like to get away from its hustle and bustle and politics every now and then myself. Your plantation looks splendid. I should like to see all of it in the morning, if I may."

"Certainly, Mrs. Lee, it would be a delight to show you around."

"I expect you will be very busy, my dear girl. I'd be happy if one of your brothers escorted myself and General Lee."

"My brothers?"

"We met them at the rail station. They may not be cavalry but they are fine horsemen and are with the rearguard of this small cavalcade. You will see them presently. You didn't know they were coming, my dear?"

Sarah had one hand to her mouth. "I had no idea."

"Well, I would guess you have many surprises yet to come."

"Why do you say that?"

"Miss Sarah!" A second coach pulled up to the mansion. Riding beside it was Jeb Stuart. He doffed his wide-brimmed hat with a flourish. "May I present my wife, Flora Stuart?"

A woman peered from the coach window. "Good evening, Miss Sarah. I so look forward to your wedding. I tire of war news day after day, even if it is about the success of Southern arms. Gowns and candles and brides and grooms will be a welcome relief."

Mrs. Lee stood with her arm through her husband's. "I agree entirely, Flora. And a Valentine's Day wedding at that."

"I'd forgotten. What a treat."

Cleveland opened her door and she stepped out.

"Sarah!" Her brother Warren rode up, jumping out of the saddle, scooping her up, and swinging her in a circle in his arms. "Did you forget all about me?"

"Oh!" She hugged her brother with a fierce strength. "How I've missed you. Where are Sam and Chris?"

"Right behind me."

Two more horses galloped up. Samuel and Christopher sprang down and each of them gave their sister a hug. She held her two younger brothers' hands.

"How on earth did you pair find the time to grow up?" she asked. "Warren looks much the same but you two look like something from *Jack and the Beanstalk.*"

"More cheerful and more friendly giants than that one, I hope," replied Sam with a grin.

"Yes," laughed Chris, "we work hard at being the sort of giants you can give a bed for the night. Of course when we face the Yankees on the battlefield we are a different sort of giant altogether."

"We are." Sam kissed Sarah on the cheek. "Whole regiments have fled from the sight of us. Why, we have our own special flag, and when it's hoisted the blue bellies turn and run for Washington."

"That won't help them much longer," Chris spoke up. "We'll have Lincoln and the capital before the year's out."

"We will. George Pickett'll see to that. He's so torn up that we hardly did anything at Fredericksburg he may get us to march on Washington by ourselves."

Sarah swung her brothers' hands. "What's this? Are you in General Pickett's division now?"

"We were transferred to Lewis Armistead's brigade in the fall," the two brothers said at the same time.

"And that's in Pickett's division," added Sam. "We've been with the brigade and the division since October."

Sarah turned to her older brother. "Who are you with, Warren?"

"I'm still with uncle's brigade. No transfer for me. I would never leave the Stonewall Brigade except in a pine box."

"Hush." Sarah put her fingers to Warren's lips. "Don't joke about such a thing."

"God's blessing on Seven Oaks." Uncle Thomas rode up with a cluster of staff officers. *"I was glad when they said unto me, Let us go into the house of the Lord."*

He removed his hat and recited the rest of the psalm.

Our feet shall stand within thy gates, O Jerusalem.

Jerusalem is builded as a city that is compact together:

Whither the tribes go up, the tribes of the Lord, unto the testimony of Israel, to give thanks unto the name of the Lord.

For there are set thrones of judgment, the thrones of the house of David.

Pray for the peace of Jerusalem: they shall prosper that love thee.

Peace be within thy walls, and prosperity within thy palaces.

For my brethren and companions' sakes, I will now say, Peace be within thee.

Because of the house of the Lord our God I will seek thy good.

"Oh, uncle." Sarah flashed him her brightest smile. "This is hardly the house of the Lord."

"Why, it is, it is indeed, for God's servants dwell within, day and night, and they make it a citadel of righteousness."

"You honor my humble estate, uncle, but it is an exaggeration just the same." She pointed. "Finally a proper uniform instead of your old schoolteachers' blue one."

Her uncle dismounted. "I should still be wearing that uniform but for my men fretting I'd be mistaken for a Yankee and shot." He nodded with his bearded chin at Stuart who had also dismounted. "Yet the greater blame for the retirement of the venerable blue coat and pants lies with General Stuart there. He said I did not comport myself like a general and bought this uniform as a gift both for myself and for the Army of Northern Virginia. I suppose it makes all the difference in the world and my men fight all the harder because of it."

"It does make all the difference in the world," said Stuart, taking his wife's hand.

"I agree." Sarah clapped her hands. "I especially like the gold braid on the sleeves. You look every inch a commander in the greatest army of our nation."

Her uncle snorted. "You sound just like Jeb. I am surrounded."

She threw her arms around her uncle. "Yes, you are. Welcome back to Seven Oaks."

He returned the hug. "I am looking forward to the marriage very much. I came directly from my headquarters in the field. Mrs. Jackson is not well or she would have made the journey here."

"Oh, no. I hadn't heard that. I hope it is nothing serious with Aunt Mary."

"Not at all, but prayer is always welcome. It is just a bout of sickness to do with the childbirth in November. I am convinced of that."

"I hope she is resting."

"She is. Or what she calls resting which others might call double time."

"What about your daughter? How is Julia Laura getting along?"

"By all accounts, splendidly. Almost three months and healthy as a Virginia cavalry colt."

"I so look forward to seeing her. I have every intention of traveling to your home in the spring."

"You will do me one better then, my dear. I haven't been home since the war began. While I did not think it would be over in 1861 like many others, I do confess I thought 1862 would see it draw to a satisfactory conclusion, with Washington suing for peace and the South carrying on with its God-given destiny." He looked at Generals Stuart and Lee. "My prayer is that this year will be the year for that."

"I pray that prayer with you," said Lee.

"Gentlemen, it will come to pass." Stuart grinned. "Even with their hard bottoms the Yankees can only take so many lickings. A couple more trips to the woodshed and they'll be bawling for peace."

"Shh, Jeb." His wife squeezed his arm and smiled. "You sound like a rustic."

"Why, I was born at Laurel Hill Farm so I come by that metaphor honestly, Mrs. Stuart."

"Shh, now. We get your drift, Jeb."

Sarah ran her hand over the face and neck of her uncle's horse. "How is Little Sorrel?"

"My gelding leads a charmed life. No enemy bullets shall strike me so long as I am on his back."

"Who told you that?"

He smiled. "It was so prophesied. We shall see. So far the prophet seems to have told the truth. I come away from my engagements with nary a scratch."

"Amen to that." Stuart indicated the brightly lit lane with a movement of his head. "Here comes the man of the hour."

Malcolm rode up with the last of the cavalry escort, leading a milk white mare by the reins. "Has anyone seen a beautiful bride hereabouts? I've scoured the back roads between here and Maryland and I greatly fear the Yankees may have her."

Sarah left her uncle and hurried up to Malcolm as he reined his horse in. "No Yankee has me. Don't you look dashing? Have you stolen your commanding general's sash and feather?"

"I haven't. It's my own. His is yellow but mine is red like the redlined cape you gave me." He touched his hat. "My brim is turned up like his, it's true, but my feather is that of Virginia's red-tailed hawk, it is not one from an ostrich, and while the flower in my lapel may be as red as General Stuart's, it is always a rose, never anything less."

Stuart shrugged. "I take such red flowers as come my way. Captain Ross is much more particular about the matter."

"Why all the red?" asked Sarah.

"I might ask you the same thing, my lady," replied Malcolm.

She glanced down at her scarlet dress. "You have often told me I look becoming in red."

"I have not changed my mind. Though I will take white tomorrow afternoon."

"I am glad to hear it. But that still does not explain your own fondness for wearing crimson. I certainly never told you that you were becoming in that hue."

"No, you didn't. But there is a Scottish poem that my ancestors loved. And I thought, well, go into battle like that, go into battle like a clansman and a Scottish prince and a cavalier of Virginia."

"My goodness, something has got you excited, Malcolm Beckett Ross. I hope it's me and not some odd legend from the misty isles."

"It so happens it is you." Malcolm sat straighter in the saddle and struck a pose.

O my Love's like a red, red rose

That's newly sprung in June
O my Love's like the melody
That's sweetly played in tune.
As fair art thou, my bonnie lass
So deep in love am I
And I will love thee still, my dear
Till all the seas gang dry
Till all the seas gang dry, my dear
And the rocks melt with the sun
I will love thee still, my dear
While the sands of life shall run.
And fare thee well, my only Love
And fare thee well, a while!
And I will come again, my Love
Though it were ten thousand mile.

Stuart clapped his hands. "A true cavalier just like his general."

"Well, that is quite a way for the bridegroom to arrive, I declare." The white mare was nuzzling Sarah and she rubbed the mare's forehead. "Are you going to tell me about this exquisite horse? Is it booty from the Yankees like Little Sorrel was?"

"Not at all. I surely hate to make a long story short, especially when it's a good one, but I saved the mother from a swamp of mud it was sinking down into. She couldn't get herself loose and she was screaming to high heavens. The farmer had his gun and was going to shoot her when I rode up. Got a rope around her and Tempest and I pulled her loose after a fair bit of effort. The old man was so grateful he gave me one of the mare's colts, this two year old filly named Cotton." Malcolm extended the reins to Sarah. "She's yours."

"Mine? You can't be serious, Malcolm."

"I hear there's a wedding. Folks have come from as far away as Richmond and Winchester and the guest list includes Generals Robert E. Lee and James Ewell Brown Stuart, not to mention the infamous Stonewall Jackson. I thought I'd best get my hand in while I can. I don't guess anyone's given you a wedding gift like this as of yet."

"Of course they haven't."

"Well, then, that makes me the best man, doesn't it?"

"Oh, Malcolm, it doesn't make you the best man. It makes you the groom. You win the bride. If I had any doubts about marrying you before this evening they have all vanished in the breeze."

"Well, then, that sounds like the best man to me."

Sarah laughed, the mare nipping at her gown. "You are stubborn. All right, you're the first best man. Whoever stands with you tomorrow is the second best man."

"That's more to my liking."

Stuart lifted a gauntleted hand. "I think a swift ride around the Yankee army should be the first order of the evening for the bride and groom. Tomorrow will be too busy for that. The moon is on the wane so the night will be jeweled with stars."

"The Yankee army?" repeated Jackson.

"The plantation will do in its stead. Certainly Sarah can't possibly sit still and be our hostess for the evening before she has run the white mare."

Jackson smiled in the lantern light, his eyes gleaming and his thick beard lined with amber. "I expect you're right."

"Please ensure that the mare is suitable." Stuart half-bowed to Sarah. "You may tell us all about it at the evening meal."

"That's very gracious," responded Sarah, "but I can't leave Seven Oaks while I have guests."

"You won't be leaving it. You'll be riding around it. Keeping an eye on things. Defending us." Stuart tipped his hat. "Please."

Sarah looked to her uncle and General Lee.

Lee smiled a soft smile. "If my daughter were given such a gift I should like to see her put the horse through its paces straightaway."

"Go indoors and change, my dear," added Mrs. Lee. "I'm sure your servants and your brothers will see us well taken care of until your return."

"We will indeed," said Warren. "Billy King. Cleveland. Bring the baggage in from the coaches."

"Yes, sir," replied Cleveland.

"What about the troopers, sir?" asked Billy King.

"The boys will find the hayloft almost as good as a feather bed. They may use our barns and stables."

"All right, sir."

Sarah was hurrying up the steps into the house behind General Lee and his wife. She glanced back at the cavalrymen. "I want them served the same fare we will be dining on, Billy King."

"Yes, Miss Sarah."

"And bring out stacks of woolen blankets for the men to use."

"I will."

"My boys can sleep on rocks," said Stuart. "And thrive on raw bacon."

"But we like good Southern food and good Southern hospitality as much as you do, General," spoke up one of his troopers with a grin.

"I know you do." Stuart winked at Sarah who had paused in the doorway. "Plenty of Virginia ham for my boys, and bacon and grits and sweet potatoes. Go on and kill the fatted calf, Miss Sarah. You're only going to get married once."

"That's true, General Stuart," she replied. "The fatted calf it is." She turned to Billy King who was bringing the Lee's luggage up the steps to the porch. "When we sit down to our meal, keep feeding those Virginia boys until they surrender."

"I'll do that, Miss Sarah."

She changed her outfit and dashed back to Malcolm's side in a riding skirt and jacket. He had placed a cavalry saddle on Cotton and they disappeared into the dark. Away from the lanterns, Sarah discovered that Jeb Stuart had been right. A bright moon was nowhere to be seen and the clear skies throbbed with stars.

"How is the mare?" asked Malcolm.

"Why, smooth as cream."

"She's hardly been ridden. But the farmer assured me she was a lamb."

"I wouldn't say lamb. I can tell she has plenty of spirit. But at the same time she is good-natured."

Malcolm reined in Tempest. "Just like someone else I know."

Sarah brought Cotton up beside him. "And who is that?"

Malcolm leaned over and kissed her on the lips. "My firebrand, the most beautiful woman in Virginia."

"You exaggerate, sir."

"She can be the flames in the Franklin stove one moment and soft as starlight in another. As a matter of fact, the silver of the starlight that is straying upon us right now is as becoming when it mixes with your hair and your figure as the scarlet gown you were wearing when I arrived."

She smiled. "I think being a cavalier has made you more gallant than you were before, if that's possible."

"I love to pay you compliments. Can you blame me? But not one of them is insincere."

He leaned over from his saddle and kissed her again.

She put a leather-gloved hand to his cheek. "We must remember our guests and the meal that needs to be served."

"Your kisses are all I need. I have no hunger pangs at all when your lips are pressed to mine."

He put one arm around her, lifted her out of her saddle, and placed her in his. She was so surprised she could not get a word out before his mouth covered hers and both arms tightened about her back and shoulders. She ran her hands over his uniform and felt the strength and the muscles underneath. A surge of happiness went through her like summer lightning.

"I love you," she whispered.

"Tomorrow will be the greatest day of my life," he responded, tugging the cavalry gauntlet from his hand and running a finger along her chin.

"I feel the same way. I just wish my father and mother could have been here to witness it."

"I know. But thank goodness your brothers are with us."

"I am grateful for that." She kissed him on the cheek. "Thanks to you and the other soldiers the war will be over soon. I have high hopes that all my brothers will return to Seven Oaks alive and well."

"You think it will be over soon?"

"Isn't that what you said when you came galloping in here? Isn't that what the generals and my brothers said? Isn't that what the Richmond papers are saying all the time?"

He cradled her against his chest and took a long look at the stars and constellations. "I was in high spirits. And when I'm in high spirits I believe anything I want to believe. Some days I'm like everyone else in the Confederacy – we're winning, and we're going to keep on winning, and one day very soon the war will be won."

"What would make you think otherwise?"

"The Yankees are fighting better, for one thing. Your uncle knows that. He has the highest regard for the Northerners' Iron Brigade that's made up of men from Michigan and Indiana and Wisconsin. He faced off against them at Gainesville and South Mountain and Sharpsburg and they were tough as spikes each time. The Irish Brigade men are holy terrors too once they unfold those green flags of theirs. The Yankees are toughening up right down the line and that includes their cavalry, Sarah, I see that plain as day. I still believe we'll whip them but when I'm in a more reflective mood I'm convinced it'll take longer than a few more months."

"Just because the enemy is fighting better than they used to?"

"No." He pointed. "August and February are the best months for shooting stars. Did you see that one?"

"I had my eyes closed."

"It had a tail as long as your hair. If we both see one at the same time it will be good luck."

"You've convinced me. My eyes are wide open now. Listening to you it sounds like the South will need all the luck it can get."

"It's not that bad. We have the best generals and the best officers and the best troops and cavalry. But the South's fate hinges on what happens with the Army of Northern Virginia. And that means our nation's hope rests on the shoulders of Generals Lee, Longstreet, Jackson, and Stuart for the most part. Your uncle is brilliant in the field – why, they all are. But here's the thing. Longstreet is loyal to General Lee and to the South, but he is also critical of some of the things Lee does."

"How do you know that?"

"It comes down through the officers' gossip."

"Gossip! Why, gossips would tell you Longstreet was on Lincoln's payroll."

"It's not just the gossip. I've accompanied General Stuart twice to Lee's headquarters and several times to your uncle's and once I've overheard the conversation in Longstreet's tent while I waited outside. Longstreet feels Lee is too willing to throw his men into attacks that cause high casualties. He wins the fight but our losses are great and may someday become more than we can bear."

Sarah lifted her head off his chest. "But General Lee is wonderful. Look at the victories he's given us."

"I know. He has nerves of steel and the wit of a fox. But Sharpsburg, what some of the papers call Antietam, well, that was no victory, Sarah. It was a bloodbath. And we were stopped cold. We had to withdraw. The Richmond newspapers say it was a victory or a draw. But our invasion of the North came to a dead end at Antietam Creek. We were the ones who pulled back, not the Yankees."

She could see he didn't like telling her these things but she had no wish to stop him. Not only because she wanted to hear his point of view on the war, but because he trusted her enough to tell her things she knew he'd share with no one else. It made her love for him grow. She had no intention of telling him it was enough until he made up his own mind that he'd said all he was going to say.

"I've heard it said that Longstreet feels your uncle is best when he's not directly under Lee's command," Malcolm continued. "When he's free to choose his own direction and his own plans. I've seen that. When your uncle was in the Shenandoah Valley he had a free hand and his actions were the actions of a genius. Just like they were at First Manassas." Malcolm laughed up at the stars. "Yes, genius and plain old stubbornness. But Stonewall didn't have that same freedom at South Mountain or Antietam or on the Peninsula when we were pushing the Yankees back from Richmond. Lee is very strong-willed – well, all his generals are, so he has to have an even stronger will. Gracious he may be, but his word is law. Sometimes there is room to maneuver with him. Most of the time, from what I've heard with my own ears and seen with my own eyes, once the matter is settled in his mind it must be settled in his generals' minds too. Yes, he's won great victories against tremendous odds. Yes, he's one of the reasons we're on the brink of gaining our independence. But what if he goes too far? What if he pushes too hard? What if his pride and his strength break us as much as they break Lincoln and the Yankees?"

Sarah waited several minutes before speaking. "Do you honestly think that's going to happen?"

"No, no. We love him. The whole army loves him. I shouldn't be talking like this. He's our greatest general after your uncle and a guest at your mansion to boot. He's our hope, our future, our symbol. The Yankees are afraid of him just like they're afraid of Stonewall Jackson and afraid of Jeb Stuart and his officers and his cavalry."

"His officers? You don't look scary to me."

"Oh, you should see me at full charge with my saber cutting the air to pieces and my rebel's yell like the shriek of a thousand wildcats with their tails in a twist. Even you'd run."

"I'll never run from you." She slid her arms under his. "You'll never harm me, Malcolm Beckett Ross. Quite the opposite. I know you'll always defend me and honor me."

"Yes, as God is my witness."

"Thank you for talking about all of that. It must be a load to carry with you wherever you go. Can't we pray about it before we head back? I'd like your mind to be at ease for our wedding."

He glanced up at the night sky again. "I don't tell anyone. Not anyone. I'm wrong, I'm sure I'm wrong, I'm sure I'm wringing my hands and wringing my heart for nothing. But the Bible fell open to Judges chapter five the other day and I read it and it troubled me.

Sarah, it troubled me so much I memorized it hoping that would help me understand."

And the princes of Issachar were with Deborah, even Issachar, and also Barak – he was sent on foot into the valley. For the divisions of Reuben there were great thoughts of heart.

Why abodest thou among the sheepfolds, to hear the bleatings of the flocks? For the divisions of Reuben there were great searchings of heart.

Gilead abode beyond Jordan – and why did Dan remain in ships? Asher continued on the seashore, and abode in his breaches.

Zebulun and Naphtali were a people that jeoparded their lives unto the death in the high places of the field.

The kings came and fought, then fought the kings of Canaan in Taanach by the waters of Megiddo – they took no gain of money.

They fought from heaven. The stars in their courses fought against Sisera.

The river of Kishon swept them away, that ancient river, the river Kishon. O my soul, thou hast trodden down strength.

Then were the horsehoofs broken by the means of the prancings, the prancings of their mighty ones.

Sarah felt a coldness along her spine as if someone had laid a blade of naked steel against her skin.

A moment later silver streaked across the dark and strewed sparks from north to south.

She hugged Malcolm's arm. "There. No more Captain Gloomy. We both saw it. That's the sign of good luck you were telling me about."

His smile was so small and thin she could barely see it.

"I guess prayer is my good luck," he said in a voice that was almost a whisper. "I guess you are too. If General Lee and Stonewall Jackson are the heart and soul of the South then you are the heart and soul of Malcolm Beckett Ross. You and God."

"Oh, my love, I don't believe I can live up to that."

"You can. Just keep on doing all the things you do. Remember how we weathered the storm in your mansion eighteen months ago? The rain? The flooding? The raiders? We'll keep on weathering the storm of this war too." He grasped her face gently in his fingers. "Never mind dark prophesies that may be no more than lack of sleep. Never mind comets which burn up and vanish in the heavens. Forget about conversations I've heard in houses and at campfires and standing in the cold rain by open tent flaps. Life starts again tomorrow afternoon. It's new for you and me by three o'clock. We become one flesh and everything, absolutely everything, is a fresh start. Do you believe that?"

"I want to. But I'll still be plain old Sarah Nunley with a different last name. That's the only thing that will be new, Malcolm. Please don't put a ring on my finger if you expect me to turn into someone else by nightfall."

"Therefore shall a man leave his father and his mother, and shall cleave unto his wife, and they shall be one flesh. Genesis, chapter two, and verse twenty-four. Believest thou this?"

"Oh, Malcolm, you sound like a Methodist bishop. Or my uncle."

"Believest thou this?"

"Yes, yes, I believest thou this. Whatever makes you happy."

He threw his head back and laughed. "It does, you know."

He suddenly seized and kissed her with so much fire and passion she thought she was going to go limp, slip through his hands, and fall to the ground.

"You are going to be my wife," he said, the boyish beauty back in his face. "My wife. My bride. The mother of my children. All the best things in the world rolled up into one person. I won't be able to sleep, Sarah. I swear before God, I won't be able to sleep a wink. I might as well spend my time on my knees or reading the Bible through from Genesis to Revelation for all the rest I'll get. And it's not just about our wedding night. It's about a lifetime. I have the most astonishing lifetime to look forward to with you, Sarah Nunley, the belle of Virginia and the Confederate States of America. Thank God. You may not think you're going to change. But I will. I'll change in the blink of an eye."

His enthusiasm and the light moving through his eyes made her smile. "What will you change into, my darling? You're already a dashing cavalier."

"I'll become much more than that." He kissed her lips. "I'll become your man, your man forever."

His mood steadily improved as the evening wore on and Sarah watched him enjoy the table talk during the meal. The shadows his words had placed in her mind also slipped away as she saw her uncle laugh – only Jeb Stuart seemed to be able to get him laughing like that

– and after enjoying a pleasant conversation with General Lee and his wife while they ate. The General seemed to take pleasure in the table talk as well, once more kissing her hand, this time without her wearing a cotton glove on it, and telling her before he retired that the evening had been a welcome respite.

"It is not often I can wholly take my mind off our nation's affairs," he said with his soft smile. "Seven Oaks has been a sanctuary for me this day."

"Why, thank you, General Lee," she replied. "I hope tomorrow may bless you and your lovely wife in much the same way."

"I'm sure it will. General Stuart has the highest regard for your young man, as does General Jackson. From what I have observed at the dinner table I can see why. May the Lord grant you many years of marital bliss and a fine Virginia home full of healthy and happy sons and daughters."

"That's very gracious, General Lee. You warm my heart with your words."

"I am heartily glad to hear it. I pray the richest blessings of our Lord God fall gently upon all the ladies of Virginia and the South. They have already endured too much. But I hope the end is not too far off."

"I pray for that, General Lee."

Mrs. Lee took her husband's arm with a smile. "The General would keep you up all night with his blessings and his gallantries. However a bride needs her rest before her grand entrance. Sweet dreams, my dear, and we look forward to seeing you wed to your handsome cavalier on St. Valentine's Day."

"Goodnight, Mrs. Lee. Goodnight, General. God grant you both a pleasant rest."

"I have every confidence he shall, my dear," responded Mrs. Lee. "The Lord is close to all his children."

Sarah watched them ascend the staircase to their room. Malcolm, her uncle, Jeb, her brothers, and several other officers were holding forth in the library, chatting and laughing and speaking of the army and God and horses all in the same breath. She looked in on them for a minute or two, left and hunted about for Billy King and asked after the troopers bedded down in the stables and barns, sat and conversed with Flora Stuart a half hour, and finally succumbed to Letta's and Harriet's admonitions to take to her bedchamber after wishing all her guests a pleasant night. She read from her Bible, prayed about everything she could think of to pray about, and turned down her oil lamp.

Who is she that looks forth as the morning, fair as the moon, clear as the sun, and awesome as an army with banners?

Verses from the Song of Songs ran through her head.

My beloved is like a gazelle or a young stag. Behold, he stands behind our wall, he looks forth through the windows, showing himself through the lattice. My beloved spoke, and said unto me, Rise up, my love, my fair one, and come away. For lo, the winter is past, the rain is over and gone.

Sometimes she thought she was sleeping, and in her sleep seeing Malcolm's young face as well as the faces of her mother and father and brothers, the path in the forest behind the house, and her uncle talking to her about raindrops and showers and the mysterious ways of God. Other times she was certain she was wide awake and dreaming nothing, that everything was taking place in front of her eyes.

Let me see your face, let me hear your voice, for sweet is your voice, and your countenance is lovely.

The fragrance of your breath is like apples. And the roof of your mouth like the best wine for my beloved, that goes down sweetly, flowing gently over lips and teeth.

I am my beloved's, and his desire is toward me.

Behold, you are handsome, my beloved, yes, pleasant.

My beloved is unto me as a cluster of henna blossoms in the vineyards of En Gedi.

At some point she knew she must have slept for she remembered shifting patterns of dark green and dark blue moving across her mind and an experience of deep peace. Although her imagination was a tumble of colors and images in the morning when Harriet woke her, she felt rested and the rain running down her windowpane did not stop her from smiling at the thought of what lay ahead.

You will be my husband, Malcolm, you will be my beloved. Oh, I wish the morning was over and we were already standing in front of the altar in the woods. And if the rains persist we will stand before the hearth in the library. It doesn't matter to me so long as the words are spoken and the vows taken.

Sarah did not go down for breakfast or for lunch. All morning Ellie fussed with her hair and nails, and brought in Harriet to help with eyebrows and lips and face, while Letta and two other ladies cooked. Warren rode past the window once the rain ended in the company of

General and Mrs. Lee, Jeb and Flora Stuart, and several officers and cavalrymen. It was just about eleven o'clock. She had no idea where her uncle was but then she remembered it was up to him to bring in the minister from the Presbyterian church several miles away.

"You are perfection, Miss Sarah," said Harriet. "Now for the bone skirt. Six or eight?"

Sarah looked at herself in the long oval mirror and made a face, the *tomboy face,* her mother used to call it. "I can't abide eight bones. It makes me feel like an oversized parasol."

"Now, Miss Sarah."

"If I wear eight bones the slightest puff of wind will scoop me up and carry me to China."

"Six bones it is."

Sarah extended her hands towards the ceiling and Ellie dropped the skirt down over her head.

"Now the wedding gown," announced Harriet. The long white gown was draped in her brown hands. "Oh, my, my, it looks so fine even without y'all in it, Miss Sarah, I expect it will be the sun, moon, and stars once it's resting on your pretty figure."

"You exaggerate, Harriet. Everyone in this household exaggerates when it comes to me."

"No one can exaggerate when it comes to you. Help me out now, Ellie."

The two women lifted the wedding dress over Sarah like a crown. She stretched her arms to the ceiling once again and they carefully lowered it down over her body and hoop skirt. Then they quickly smoothed it into place over her arms and back and stomach.

Harriet pressed the heel of a palm into one of her eyes. "If your mother could see you. If she could see you all grown up and beautiful and a bride." She brushed at her other eye with her fingers. "It ain't fair and it ain't right, but lots of times life ain't fair and right. We want it to be heaven and now and then it is. But lots of the time it sure isn't."

Sarah's own eyes were burning and her throat tightening. "Maybe she can see. Maybe papa too. Maybe they all can."

Her uncle knocked on her door at exactly one o'clock in the afternoon. Harriet opened the door. The stern business-like look on his face melted away once he saw his niece in her white gown. He bowed and extended the crook of his arm.

"You are radiant, my dear," he said. "Come. Let us astonish your neighbors and guests."

She slid her arm through his. "Is everything ready? Is there an altar in the forest by the oaks? Did you bring the minister? Are there seats for the elderly?"

"Virginia is ready."

"And Malcolm?"

"He had thoughts of riding off with you after the ceremony. I have posed sentries at all points of the plantation. You will not get through my picket line."

"Surely he was joking, Uncle Thomas."

A smile made its way through her uncle's thick beard. "Cavalrymen are capable of performing the wildest deeds."

He walked her downstairs and out the front door. Dozens of slaves stood with their masters' carriages and horses. They doffed their caps and bowed as Sarah made her way down the steps.

"I set ours free as you did, uncle."

"I know."

"I pay them fair wages now."

"I know. I am proud of you in so many things, oh, how often I boast in the Lord when it comes to my niece Sarah. But what you have done with your household servants and field hands is very fine. The Lord is mightily pleased. The New South will soon have no more room for this institution. It will all be as it is in Paul's letter to Philemon – the slaves shall be our brothers in Christ and freemen both in body and soul. That, it seems to me, is the right direction for our entire nation to follow."

"But slavery is enshrined in the Confederate constitution, uncle."

"Enshrined, is it?" rumbled Jackson. "Well, then, we shall have to help it off its throne, won't we?" He patted her hand as it rested on his arm and gray uniform sleeve. "Let us not speak of this now. Look at how brightly the sun shines through the oak trees. Look at how green the grass is. How many times did you and I walk this very path when you were a little girl?"

She smiled and leaned her head on his shoulder. "I dreamed of the raindrop game last night. You were telling me God had sent us showers and blessed both our nation and myself. *No more raindrops,* you said, *the heavens have opened and poured forth their abundance.*"

"You dreamed that? Well, it sounds about right. Now, do you see all the people who have come to wish you God speed and offer you their prayers?"

Hundreds of men, women, and children stood under the trees or sat on the few chairs and benches made available for the elderly or the ill. A table had been draped with a white cloth and a bronze cross set in its middle. All around the cross were strewn long-stemmed red roses. The Presbyterian minister stood in front of the table in his robe. On one side were Malcolm and her three brothers. On the other, three young women from nearby plantations and from church who were childhood friends. Lucy Nightingale, her oldest girlfriend, was standing as her maid of honor. It seemed to her that her uncle's strength lifted her off the path so that she was floating to Malcolm like a swan.

My beloved is like a bouquet of henna blossoms in my arms. His eyes are for me.

His eyes were indeed fixed on her. So were everyone else's. Sarah had never been vain but she knew the dress enhanced everything about her that was womanly – her figure, her bearing, her posture, her walk, her long hair now fashioned into ringlets. Mrs. Hannicott had taken dozens of small diamonds Sarah's mother had bequeathed to her and sewn them into various parts of the wedding gown. The gems had entered the family before the *Mayflower* and been brought over from the Old World in an oak and leather casket. Now they flashed and sparked as the sun found them while she drew nearer and nearer to the altar.

Malcolm was not supposed to speak but he did anyways. "My love, you are the most beautiful creature on the face of the earth. You absolutely dazzle me. I cannot see."

She could not resist. "If you cannot see I hope you will not miss when it comes time to kiss your bride."

"I do not need eyes to find my way to your lips."

Sarah saw the minister smile and she burst into a fiery blush that covered her face in seconds.

Dearly beloved, we are gathered together here in the sight of God, and in the face of this congregation, to join together this man and this woman in holy matrimony; which is an honorable estate, instituted of God in the time of man's innocence, signifying unto us the mystical union that is betwixt Christ and his Church; which holy estate Christ adorned and beautified with his presence, and first miracle that he wrought, in Cana of Galilee; and is commended of Saint Paul to be honorable among all men: and therefore is not by any to be enterprised, nor taken in hand, unadvisedly, lightly, or wantonly, to satisfy men's carnal lusts and appetites, like brute beasts that have no understanding; but reverently, discreetly, advisedly, soberly, and in the fear of God; duly considering the causes for which matrimony was ordained.

She watched a robin fly past as she listened to the minister recite the words.

Ah, a robin! An early spring and the new beginning Malcolm so desperately wants us to be part of.

"Miss Nunley?"

She blinked. "Yes, Reverend?"

"I ask again, *Wilt thou have this man to thy wedded husband?*"

"Of course. Yes. I will."

"Who giveth this woman to be married to this man?"

Sarah thought her uncle was going to salute or draw his sword. "I do, on behalf of her dearly departed mother and father and her entire family, wherever they abide and wherever they may be found."

He relinquished her right hand and gave it to Malcolm.

"Honor her, sir," Jackson said. "She is precious in the Lord's sight and in mine."

Malcolm bowed his head. "I shall do so with the last measure of my strength, General."

Jackson nodded, kissed Sarah on the cheek, and withdrew.

I, Malcolm Beckett Ross, take thee Sarah Nunley, to my wedded wife, to have and to hold from this day forward, for better for worse, for richer for poorer, in sickness and in health, to love and to cherish, till death us do part, according to God's holy ordinance; and thereto I plight thee my troth.

I, Sarah Nunley, take thee Malcolm Beckett Ross, to my wedded husband, to have and to hold from this day forward, for better for worse, for richer for poorer, in sickness and in health, to love, cherish, and to obey, till death us do part, according to God's holy ordinance; and thereto I give thee my troth.

Sarah was certain he would not have a gold ring. But Warren handed it to him and in a gleam of light he placed it upon the ring finger of her left hand. His eyes never leaving hers, while with one ear she listened to blackbirds calling back and forth to each other in high excitement over something or other, he said, *With this ring I thee wed, with my body I thee worship, and with all my worldly goods I thee endow: In the Name of the Father, and of the Son, and of the Holy Ghost. Amen.*

"Amen," said Jackson, Lee, and Stuart at the same time.

The minister nodded at Malcolm.

Malcolm cupped Sarah's face in his hands.

"Look at you," he said, "look at you."

She smiled. "Look at both of us."

"There never was such a day since Genesis. There never was such a day since our forefathers came to America. There hasn't been anything like it since our nation was founded in 1861."

"I believe you."

"Ahem." It was Jeb Stuart. "One thing for sure that hasn't happened in Virginia is Malcolm Beckett Ross the husband kissing Sarah Beckett Ross the wife. May all of your witnesses be treated to that distinct and honorable pleasure before the sun sets on the Old Dominion today?"

Laughter made its way through the crowd and Sarah recognized her uncle's rough chuckle immediately. Blushing again, as if she were standing in a stove, she tilted her face up towards Malcolm and felt her husband's strong arms go around her back and his lips cover hers as softly and warmly as sunlight.

"In God's green earth, there never was such a beauty as you," he whispered.

Raindrops

Monday, March 9th, 1863

"Y'all understand it ain't you we wants to get away from, Mrs. Nunley Beckett Ross?"

"I know that, Jimmy Buck. Please call me Mizz Sarah."

"It's just we wants to be free wherever we go, not just on this here plantation."

"I understand that perfectly."

"Why, way up north slaves like me and Cleveland can even vote. Can you imagine that, Mizz Sarah? We can vote."

"That's something, that's truly something." Sarah looked from Jimmy Buck to Cleveland as they stood in front of the mansion. A break in the thick gray clouds lined their features in silver light. "Do you both have enough water and food for the road?"

Cleveland nodded. "You fixed us up proper. There ain't nothing more we have need of."

"The papers I wrote out for you? The ones assuring any reader that you are freemen and no longer slaves? They are on your persons?"

Cleveland patted his chest. "Tied right to me underneath my shirts. They's always gonna be with me. I thank God for 'em, Mizz Sarah. I thank God for you."

Jimmy Buck smiled. "We both do. You're a wonder and a fine, fine lady."

Sarah folded her hands in front of her. "Thank you. You have served my family and Seven Oaks well. I pray you may be safe on your journey. Mind you avoid our boys. They will think you're runaways and shoot you if they can't catch you."

"We'll be sly." Jimmy Buck removed his hat. "What with your uncle and Bobby Lee the South is bound to win the war. Everyone expects it. So we gots to go."

"I'm sure that's true. Our independence is just about within our grasp. But it will take a while to rid the New South of slavery. That is why I do not think poorly of either of you for leaving."

"We was determined to stay on for the wedding and see you set up proper after your honeymoon."

"You did. You did all of that. I'm grateful to the two of you."

"Would you pray for us before we go, Mizz Sarah?" asked Jimmy Buck.

"Of course. If General Jackson were here he would be proud to do the honors and look the other way once you took to the woods."

After her blessing, Jimmy Buck returned his hat to his head, nodded, and made his way around the side of the house and into the forest. Cleveland lingered, his eyes fixed on Sarah, but a half minute later he joined Jimmy Buck. Sarah remained standing at the foot of the steps to the porch. She was thinking of how the two had served at her wedding. This was followed by memories of dancing first with Malcolm, followed by her uncle, Stonewall Jackson, who was in turn followed by General Lee.

Bobby Lee was quite the gentleman dancer. He did not have the young man's glide or my uncle's intensity but he was very regal in his movements. It was quite pleasant. After that it was my brothers. I dreaded going about our ballroom with them. I was certain their waltzing would still be awkward. But they had grown into men while they were soldiers. It could not have been due to practice. No one dances on the picket line with other men or even in a winter camp when there can be so much boredom. It can only mean they have come by it naturally. Won't their ladies be blessed when the days come for them both to begin courting?

More memories slipped through her mind.

She was at the punch bowl and Malcolm was tipping a cup against her lips a little too quickly and the pink contents of the crystal glass splashed over her throat. For a moment she was afraid he was going to kiss her skin clear of the punch and scandalize everyone in the ballroom, but he only bowed, apologized, and offered her his handkerchief, which she used to pat the pink liquid from her neck and throat.

She managed to elude her guests and step out onto the lawn for air. For two minutes she was on her own, breathing in the cool February night mist, dreaming of what was to come when she was finally alone with her husband, before a soft kiss on the nape of her neck made her jump. She was so startled she swung around to slap whoever had done it, not considering that only one man would dare. Malcolm caught her gloved hand in mid-strike, put it to his lips, winked, pulled her in close, and moved his lips from her hand to her mouth, covering it, and prolonging the kiss until she felt she was a sheet of flame.

"Why can't we run away now?" she whispered.

"I'd like nothing better," he replied, also whispering, "but when we have guests like Bobby Lee and Jeb Stuart, not to mention your illustrious uncle, it simply can't be done. Well, perhaps if we were Yankees we might do it. But we are both Virginians and we have a code to follow the rest of the world knows nothing about."

"That may well be, Malcolm Beckett Ross, but it seems criminal to me to keep a young lady waiting, and that is something a Virginia gentleman ought never to do either."

"How have I kept you waiting?"

She finally got her slap in, smacking him on the cheek, but it was playful and light. "How? You ask your bride how? I wish to turn down the sheets of my wedding bed and welcome you to my arms. So far I have waited more than five hours for that opportunity. And it is a God-given opportunity, I might remind you."

"I know it is. But we are encumbered by custom."

"Oh, drat all the wedding customs and Southern expectations. Can't you go back in there, make an announcement, and whisk me away?"

"Very soon I may."

She put her hands on slender hips covered by an equally slender white bridal gown. "Two hours doesn't suit me, Malcolm." She reached out with white-gloved fingers and traced his lips. "Don't you want to be alone with me?"

"More than anything."

"Anything? More than riding with Jeb Stuart?"

"Yes, certainly."

"More than stealing horses from the Yankees?"

"Unquestionably."

"More than sitting down with my uncle and staring at battle maps?"

He grinned his young boy grin. "Well, perhaps not that, my dear."

The playful slap struck again.

He swept her up off the ground, laughing.

She squealed and covered her mouth with her hand, laughing harder than he was.

"All right, Sarah," he announced, striding across the lawn with her. "You win. Let's be on our way."

She twined her arms about his neck. "Just like that? I win?"

"Indeed you do. I surrender unconditionally."

He placed her in a carriage, its horse already waiting and tethered to a post.

"This is ours?" she asked.

"It is. But since you can't wait another hour, and since you have challenged my Virginia manhood, I must do what any Southern gentleman would do – spirit you away."

At Malcolm's request, Cleveland and Jimmy Buck ushered the guests out of the ballroom and onto the porch and drive, holding flaming torches high over their heads. Malcolm took her by the hand and she alighted momentarily from the carriage, doing a sort of curtsey as raindrops began to drop on her shoulders and gown. Malcolm bowed to the crowd of soldiers and civilians.

"I expect we should stay longer," he announced in a loud voice. "But there are many demands upon my time. Virginia makes demands, our Southern nation makes demands, why, even the gallant General Jeb Stuart makes demands."

"And so I should!" Stuart cried back. "You just have to tip your hat and the Yankee horses and supply wagons flow in your direction! I can't spare you!"

Malcolm raised his hand as laughter swirled about them. "Nevertheless, the demands of married life call louder than the cavalry bugle or the clash of swords or the creaking wheels of Yankee carts piled high with food and ammunition. So I must do my duty and bid you all a fond farewell. *Adieu, adieu,* and *adieu.*"

He helped her back into the carriage, untethered the reins, jumped into the driver's seat, clicked his tongue, and steered them along the dark drive and through the trees that were dripping with water. They both waved until the night took them away. A cottage on his parents' plantation had been decorated for the occasion and they'd spent their honeymoon there, never disturbed, their meals brought quietly to them by slaves Malcolm had grown up with and who he trusted with his life. It had been idyllic. As Sarah closed her eyes, still at the spot where she had stood when she saw Cleveland and Jimmy Buck walk into the woods, she lifted her face to the heavens and let a sudden shower wet her through completely, her mind still at the honeymoon cottage and the long walks with her husband along hidden pathways. It felt to her as if she were being baptized, in some special way, by God himself.

It is the beginning of my new life. It is the beginning of our new country.

Friday, March 20th

Tap. Tap. Tap. Tap.

Sarah was asleep but she heard the tapping sound. She knew it was rain on her window pane, knew she was hearing it as she slept, knew that in her dream it was the tapping of hooves against cobblestone, was aware she was both awake and sleeping at the same time, and decided to stay under her covers and continue to let the beautiful black horse walk through her imagination, the rider a man she did not recognize but who seemed friendly enough.

Clop. Clop. Clop. Clop.

Sarah opened her eyes.

That was not the tapping of raindrops.

Letta knocked quietly on her door. "Mizz Sarah? Are you up?"

"Who is here? Is it my husband?"

"It's your uncle, Mizz Sarah. He said to tell you he brings dispatches."

"Dispatches! He means letters from Malcolm!"

"He mentioned your brothers, Mizz Sarah – Warren, Christopher, and Sam."

"Oh, no, he's not going to get away with that sort of teasing, Letta. I know he wouldn't stop by Seven Oaks unless he had something special for me. Yes, my brothers are special, but he knows I long for news of the man I married. Why, it's scarcely been a month since we were wed."

"I know, Mizz Sarah."

"It's silly for us to be talking through a door. Come in and help me get dressed."

"Yes, ma'am."

Letta brushed out Sarah's hair, helped her into a six bone skirt and pale yellow dress, tied yellow ribbons in her hair, and went downstairs to see how her uncle and his officers were getting on while Sarah sat at the vanity and applied her makeup. When Sarah came down to the parlor her uncle and the six officers with him all stood.

"The Flower of Virginia." Her uncle raised his cup of coffee. "I thank God you are looking so fine."

"And I thank you for your gallantry. Welcome to Seven Oaks, gentlemen. I trust we are taking care of your every need?"

An officer held up a roll covered in jam. "Blackberry too. My favorite. Blessings on this plantation, Mrs. Ross."

"You're most welcome. I assume you officers were not riding on your own?"

"The troopers are in the kitchen, all twenty of them." Her uncle and the officers were still standing. "We know all too well how you feel about such things from previous visits."

"I am glad to hear it. Please sit down, gentlemen. Thank you for your courtesy."

They all sat down except her uncle.

"Come with me," he invited her. "Stretching my legs will do me good."

She followed him out the back door and down the path through the trees, slipping her arm through his once they reached the oak trees.

"How are you feeling?" she asked him.

"I thank our Lord; I haven't felt better in my life. The whole army is in the same frame of mind as I am. The North will hear from Virginia this spring and summer."

"We all expect this to be the end and that our borders will be secure and inviolate by Christmas and the Yankees gone. Do we hope for too much?"

"If one hopes in God one never hopes for too much."

"I do hope in God. All of Virginia does."

"Then we do what we are able to do and leave it in God's hands. I pray that 1863 will be the consummation of all our prayers and wishes but I cannot presume to dictate to the

Almighty. His ways are beyond our ways, his plans eternal and unfathomable. Of course he may offer us a revelation. Certainly our army felt that way when we saw the Northern Lights flame over our victorious battlefield at Fredericksburg in December. However I require something more, a passage of Scripture, a holy phrase from a holy sermon that tugs at my mind and my spirit and which will not go away. Nevertheless I also have my hopes. Let us lick the North another time or two and the war will be done and the lines for Virginia fall in pleasant places." He stopped walking and stared up at the tall oaks, most of which were showing fresh green. "It's the first day of spring, isn't it? Campaigning will begin soon, my dear. We have our eyes on Joe Hooker and the Army of the Potomac. Lincoln will pressure him to attack. Once we deal with that General Lee and I are convinced we must head north again as we did last fall. This time we expect a more fruitful outcome."

"Is General Stuart on the move?"

"Somewhat." He bent and kissed her on the cheek. "Come. No more waiting. I have a letter in my pocket. " He gave it to her. "Please feel free to read it while I wait."

"Are you sure?"

"I am."

He stepped away a few feet, hands behind his back, continuing to look at the spring oaks and, Sarah was sure, meditate on the words of God that constantly ran through his mind.

My love

I dash this off in my saddle as I am going one way and your uncle another. I am not revealing any great military secrets when I say nothing big is up at the moment. But once the roadways begin to dry we will be on the move in force and the Yankees too. I welcome it. Let us settle this thing and let me be back in your sweet and tender arms again. I miss you, how I miss you. I ache for your kisses. God knows I will have no peace until your lips are sweet against mine again.

Always and forever
Your Malcolm

Sarah read the letter twice and then folded it back into its envelope.

Her uncle smiled. "Good news?"

"It's always good news when I hear from Malcolm. He could tell me he had a stomach ache and I would be happy just to see his words scribbled across the page."

"Hm." He glanced up at the treetops again. "Do you remember when we used to play raindrops?"

"I do."

"We should try that again for a few minutes."

"All right." She paused a moment, waiting on him, but when he said nothing she spoke up. "A small army with small numbers. But it wins great victories many didn't expect it could win."

Jackson had returned his cavalry gauntlets to his hands and pulled gloved fingers through his beard. "Like Gideon's small army."

"Just like. And it was God who made sure it was small too."

"Yes. It proved to others that the might of Gideon's army came from God himself."

"I feel the same way about the army of Northern Virginia."

"Well, I feel the same way about you, my dear."

"Me? What have I done?"

"You were a young girl here among these oak trees. You used to hide from me. We spoke of God and the wonders of life and quoted Scripture verses to each other. Why, you were no taller than a rabbit. Now you are a married woman. In due time you shall have children of your own. You are mistress of Seven Oaks and have managed it with equal measures of dignity, grace, and strength. So small, you were once so small, a cloud in the distance no greater than the size of a man's hand, but now you have brought showers of blessing to us all. Who would have thought it? Generals Lee and Stuart still talk of their evenings here and long to return when this year's campaign is over – oh, I pray to God, when this war is over. Even General Longstreet has confessed the wedding was a tonic, the night in the feather bed the best rest he's had since the war began."

"General Longstreet did not say that."

Jackson grunted, still tugging at his beard and glancing about at the trees. "When have you known me to exaggerate? Old Pete slept like a felled oak. His words."

Sarah decided to change the direction of the game. "I have one. A horse so small yet it does deeds so great."

"And what horse is that? General Lee's mount Traveller?"

"Come, uncle. Is Traveller so small?"

"Ha." Jackson glanced up at the gray sky, blinking as raindrops fell into his eyes. "Malcolm's horse is of a good size. So is General Stuart's."

"Perhaps you should fast and pray and then the answer will be revealed to you."

He laughed. "It's so serious a matter, is it?"

"Well, it is serious when you don't know your own horse."

"What?"

"Little Sorrel, uncle. Why, you're almost bigger than he is."

"Little Sorrel! I never think of him as small. He is calm and steady under fire and has no fear of cannonades or musket fire or the harsh shouts of fighting men."

"Which is exactly the point of the game, isn't it? He's barely fifteen hands and there you are, towering in the saddle at six feet. You ride this small mount into battle, Minie balls whistling about the two of you, and I'm sure our troops and the Yankees wonder why Little Sorrel doesn't turn tail and flee. But he never does."

"Never," growled Jackson, his eyes dark and distant, reliving for a moment a fight in another place and at another time.

"So perhaps you should have called him Raindrops, uncle. The small things that presage something greater and more momentous."

"The troops are stuck on his name now and, I confess, so am I. However I am not averse to whispering *Raindrops* into his ear now and then." He pulled a pocket watch from his pants pocket and frowned. "Ah. The hours slip away. I must head on."

"So soon?"

"War keeps its own clock."

"Here. I must send something back with you for Malcolm." She sat on a nearby bench. "Billy King!"

She knew he had been standing at the back of the house. "Yes, ma'am," he replied.

"Pray fetch me my best gold-nib pen and a pot of ink. And a fresh sheet of paper too."

"I will, ma'am."

Jackson put his hands behind his back. "Do not write an epistle. We have no time for an epistle."

"Love keeps its own clock, Stonewall Jackson."

Billy King arrived with pen, paper, and a small wooden board she placed in her lap. She wrote swiftly and smoothly, never looking up or saying a word. In five minutes she was done. She stood up, blew on the paper to dry the ink, folded it twice, took a yellow ribbon from her hair to bind it with, and handed it to her uncle.

"There you are," she said. "I trust the war is not lost."

"Hm." He tucked the letter away inside the front of his gray uniform. "I hope we may pass this way during the summer campaign. Until then I fear our attention must be directed towards Fredericksburg where Joe Hooker and the Yankee army are preparing to cause us more trouble."

She put a hand on his arm. "You will prevail. The rainstorm the North did not anticipate is about to break over their heads."

"I pray so."

"Don't doubt it." She squeezed his arm. "You will be careful. You and Malcolm."

"I don't know what that means, my dear. We are winning this war by charging ahead. All my life I have charged ahead. The small becomes the great by charging ahead."

"I am always praying."

"And so you should be for our lives are ordered by divine providence. But I am as safe in battle as I am in one of your featherbeds. God has fixed the time of my death whether at forty or fifty or a hundred, whether from a saber blow or the strike of a bullet or the final collapse of my heart. Nothing and no one can touch me unless the Lord wills it. My body and soul are in his hands." His voice quieted and he gently placed a finger to her cheek. "As are young Malcolm's."

She brushed quickly at her eyes. "Those are good hands."

"They are indeed. *The eternal God is thy refuge and underneath are the everlasting arms.*"

"Deuteronomy 33 and verse 27."

He nodded. "Raindrops."

All through spring Sarah felt like she was holding her breath and that nature was holding its breath with her.

"Sometimes," she whispered as she wrote in her diary, "I feel as if God Almighty is holding his breath too."

The work of the plantation kept her busy, the plowing and sowing and repairs to the barns and the house and the servants' quarters. She thanked God for the nights she dropped to sleep like a stone and remembered nothing that she had dreamed. But in the daylight, no matter how busy it was, the thoughts always worked into her mind that the fighting would begin again soon and that her uncle and her husband would be in the thick of it.

"Fighting has broken out near Chancellorsville," Malcolm's father told her, driving his carriage up to the door one afternoon but not alighting. "I expect there will be details in the morning editions of the Richmond papers."

Sarah rested her hand on one of the horse's flanks. "But where is Chancellorsville?"

"The inn run by George Chancellor. At the intersection of Orange Plank Road and the Orange Turnpike. Ten miles west of Fredericksburg." He flicked the traces and the two horses began to trot. "Be brave, my girl. Pray without ceasing. A fresh battle was bound to come our way. The important thing is that we win it. And that casualties are light."

The nearby chapel rang its bells two days later on Sunday morning May 3rd with news of a great victory arriving with the Sunday papers.

"General Jackson swept them, just swept them," Billy King told her when she came down the staircase. "That's what I've heard; that's what we've all heard."

At church Billy King's news was on everyone's tongue. Even the minister spoke about it from the pulpit.

"We must thank God even though the details are sketchy," he announced. "Yankee papers say they are winning the battle but they have been saying that every day since the war began."

On Monday the 4th and Tuesday the 5th the battle in and around Chancellorsville was still raging, according to the papers, but every edition confirmed that General Jackson had led a surprise attack against the Union army's right flank and routed the enemy. Praise was heaped upon his head. Sarah read the newspaper accounts again and again, her heart warm with pride that her uncle and Little Sorrel had carried the day once again. She also read that Jeb Stuart's cavalry had screened her uncle's advance as he marched his men towards the Union line. She pictured Malcolm riding his horse, tall in the saddle, saber at the ready, protecting her uncle and his troops from Yankee fire.

"I am content, Lord," she prayed. "You have brought victory to the South and I sense our independence is near. I know there is always a price to pay for freedom and I know many families have paid it. I do not want to simply celebrate our success at your hand. I want to ask you to comfort the bereaved, to be kind to the widow and orphan, to have mercy on all the families who have lost loved ones during this battle, yes, even the Northern families."

On the early morning of Wednesday, May 6th she dreamed the dream of raindrops against the windowpane again, the dream that was more than a dream because she knew she listened to real drops against real glass even as she imagined the rain falling in her sleep.

Tap. Tap. Tap. Tap.
Clop. Clop. Clop. Clop.

Hooves made her wake up completely as they always did.

She drew aside a curtain. The window was dark and the glass was dry. But a horse and rider slipped past her room.

Tap. Tap.

Her bedroom door.

"Yes?" responded Sarah. "Who is the rider?"

"One of your uncle's men." Letta's voice.

"Does he have letters or notes?"

"He said he must speak with you at once."

Sarah jumped out of bed. "I shall be down directly."

She threw on a thick housecoat, buttoned it to the top, and rushed out of her room.

The officer stood at the bottom of the stairs.

She put her hand to her mouth when she saw how black his face was from the smoke of battle and how dirt and blood was caked around his eyes and mouth.

The officer removed his hat as soon as he saw her.

"Ma'am," he announced, "your uncle is gravely wounded. We are afraid he is taking a turn for the worse and he has asked for you."

"Wounded? Badly wounded? But the papers said nothing about that."

"Will you ride with me, ma'am? Do you have a good mount? You may use a carriage if you like."

"A carriage will take too long. Where are you taking me?"

"To Orange County. To Thomas Chandler's plantation where General Jackson is being tended. He is in the office building." He wiped a hand over his eyes. "We must be careful not to take the wrong roads. The armies are still fighting."

"What about his wife?"

"I don't know. I expect messengers have been sent to her as well."

"I will get dressed for a long ride. Billy King, saddle my new mount Sugar Crest. And I want you to come with us and serve both myself and this officer."

"Yes, Mizz Sarah."

They rode for hours, sometimes stopping to rest their mounts, sometimes walking them for miles before getting back into the saddles, always trotting at a steady gait, never running the horses. Billy King had brought bread and meat and cheese and the fixings for coffee – twice he started a fire when they sat down for a few minutes to let the horses graze and brewed a pot.

"I thank you for this," the officer told him, his hands wrapped around the tin mug. "We been fighting steady since last Friday. This cup is like a gift of God."

"You're most welcome, sir," replied Billy King. "We are all grateful for your victory."

The officer stared into his coffee. "We have a victory, that's certain. But what's also certain is we have a lot of dead. Too many. I swear, too many."

Sarah reached her uncle's side in the lamplight, carrying a lantern into the plantation office building and setting it down close to his face.

"Uncle," she said softly.

His skin looked like candle wax.

"Uncle."

He opened his eyes. "Sarah. How is it you come to be here?"

His voice did not have the strength she had heard in it all her life.

"I rode. An officer brought me."

"It hurts when I breathe. It is very strange. My chest did not hurt after I was shot."

She saw that his left arm was gone. "The surgeon told me he had been forced to amputate."

"I was hit several times. It was our own troops. They thought my officers and I were Federal cavalry. Poor boys, they have taken it badly. It was dark; they didn't know. Horses were killed. Several of my officers were killed. I am blessed to have survived." He winced as he took a breath. "It is difficult to know if I will fight again."

"Of course you will." She put a hand to his forehead. "Let me get you a wet cloth. One moment."

When she returned to the room she sat by his bed and wiped his face several times.

"That feels very good," he whispered.

"You are going to be fine. How is Little Sorrel, uncle? I hope he was not hurt."

"No Minie balls struck him." He gripped her arm. "I have been reading my Bible. It gives me strength the surgeons and their medicines cannot. But my eyes are tired. Will you read to me? Perhaps it will calm my spirit enough to give me rest."

"Of course. Where is your Bible?"

"Just here by my pillow."

Sarah read Psalm 23 and one of his favorites, Psalm 18.

"*I have pursued my enemies and overtaken them, neither did I turn again until they were consumed,*" he recited along with Sarah as she read. "*For thou hast girded me with strength unto the battle, thou hast subdued under me those that rose up against me.*"

"*The Lord liveth and blessed be my rock.*" Sarah spoke the words slowly.

"*Let the God of my salvation be exalted,*" responded Jackson.

"*He delivereth me from mine enemies, yea, thou liftest me up above those that rise up against me,*" continued Sarah.

Jackson's eyes gleamed. "*Therefore will I give thanks unto thee, O Lord, among the heathen, and sing praises unto thy name.*"

He closed his eyes and slept.

Sarah sat with him a while and then went looking for the doctor. She found him sitting at a desk in another room and writing in a ledger with a quill pen.

"It hurts when he breathes," she told him.

He looked up. The candlelight moved over his face. "He has developed pneumonia. It can happen with amputations. At first we thought it was just soreness from the fall from his horse and when his stretcher was dropped during his evacuation."

"Have you caught it in time?"

"We will see, my dear. We will see. There is an empty room here with a bed you may use. I expect your slave will be comfortable with a blanket on the grass."

"He is my servant, doctor, and a free man. Thank you for all you have done."

Sarah prayed for an hour or more and was hopeful the next morning she would see rapid improvement. But although her presence animated him, and he appeared stronger when she prayed with him or read the Bible, she could see the color was slowly leaving his face and lips. By Friday he was worse and Saturday showed no improvement.

"I shall die on the Lord's Day," he said to her. "Don't be afraid. I have always wished to die on a Sunday. All these things are in his hands. I was meant to leave earth at this time and in this season. How I will miss my wife and my daughter. How I will miss my men. How I will miss you, dear Sarah. But you can come to me. All of you can come to me. I shall expect you. My Savior and I shall greet you most warmly and there will be a banquet spread for you equaling anything at Seven Oaks." He smiled a weak smile. "I shall not say it surpasses one of your feasts at the plantation."

"I – I don't want you to go, uncle. You have been with me all my life. I shall feel so alone."

"You have the Lord. You have your brothers. Most importantly, you have Malcolm."

"No one knows where Malcolm is. No one has seen him since the third of May."

"He will turn up. A battle is a most confusing affair. He will find you before you find him. Depend on it."

"Oh, uncle, I love you; I love you so much."

He gently stroked her hair with his right hand. "We have always had an understanding you and I. Our love for one another has never diminished, praise God. It will not be absent after I am gone. Your spirit will know I live. Just as my spirit will still express my love for you and my family."

Sarah slept poorly that night. On Sunday morning her uncle was tossing and turning and muttering things that made no sense. A sharp pain entered her heart as she saw him twisting about in his bed and she finally left the room so that she did not have to watch him struggle. A shout as loud as if he were on the battlefield brought her back at a run. The doctor was leaning over him.

"He was crying out for General Hill and Major Hawks," the doctor told her. "But now he's quiet."

"He's smiling." Sarah's eyes glistened. "Oh, my sweet uncle, he's smiling. How beautiful he is."

Jackson looked past Sarah and the doctor, the smile lingering.

"Let us cross over the river," he said in a quiet voice, "and rest under the shade of the trees."

The whole room and building grew silent.

Sarah did not hear any sounds from outside. No men calling, no song birds, not even the touch of wind against the side of the building.

"He's gone now, isn't he?" she asked, tears falling along her cheeks and dropping under the collar of her dress. "Something has left us. It's too quiet and empty. Something is no longer here."

The doctor checked her uncle's heartbeat and listened for his breath.

"The General is with God," he finally said.

A Seven Oaks Christmas, 1865

Whenever Sarah thought back to her uncle's death, to his sudden silence, a confused jumble of images and scents and sounds filled her mind.

Hands pressed into her shoulder as she knelt praying by her uncle's bed.

Voices murmured in the room. One was General Lee's.

There was a smell of blood and alcohol.

She was walking away from the building and plantation, tears making everything indistinct. She was far from where her uncle lay and bodies were lined up in rows on the grass; tents for casualties had popped up everywhere.

As she walked she thought she saw her uncle's body over and over again laid out on cots inside the tents.

If her imagination took her back to that day, while she slept the screaming of men undergoing amputations made her knife into a sitting position in her bed. She could hardly get her breath.

A surgeon had seen her wandering past, thought she was a nurse, and yelled for her to come and assist.

She helped hold young men down and administer opiates while the physician's saw bit into flesh and bone.

After several hours she was taught how to suture and kept at it after lanterns were brought in.

"It's a great victory," said the voices in her head.

"But it cost us too many men," said other voices.

"We lost Stonewall Jackson." She heard those words so many times. "What's going to happen now?"

"We still got Lee and Stuart and Longstreet."

"But Stonewall was the master."

"Even without him we'll lick the Yankees again and again until they finally go back north and stay there."

"The South can't win like it's been doing without Stonewall."

"Stonewall's not our army."

"He was half our army."

Malcolm had found her asleep near a stack of blood-crusted uniforms at the side of a hospital tent.

"You're covered in blood." He kept wiping at her face with his fingers. "Are you hurt? Are you shot?"

"I'm fine, I'm fine; I was helping with the wounded, that's all, just helping with the wounded."

"You've been missing for two days."

"I couldn't do anything for my uncle so I made my way here. I don't know how."

"No one knew what to think. They took your uncle to Richmond by train and he's lying in state. Mary wanted you by her side."

"Mary?"

"Your aunt, Stonewall's wife. You saw her at the building on the Chandler plantation. She slept in one of the rooms."

"No, she didn't."

"Darling, the doctor told me she was there with her baby girl three days before your uncle died."

Sarah could not remember as Malcolm held her by the hospital tent and she could not remember Mary being at her uncle's bedside as she stood on the porch watching the rain fall on Seven Oaks months later. In her head her uncle yelled for the quartermaster to bring up warm food for the troops. There was no Aunt Mary or her daughter Julia.

"I read the Bible to him. Prayed with him. Held his hand." Sarah had finally leaned her head on Malcolm's chest. Inside the tent a man was groaning. "There was a great deal of noise and confusion once he became delirious. Perhaps Aunt Mary was there. Perhaps little Julia was in my arms. I'm trying but I don't see them. They're not there."

"All right, love, it doesn't matter; it doesn't matter at all. I'm going to help you get cleaned up and escort you to Richmond. We may still have time to see him lying in state."

"I don't want to see him lying in state. I don't want to see him lying anywhere. I've seen enough bodies."

"It's probably too late anyway. In his will he asked to be buried in Lexington so that is where we should go."

"I have no desire to see him locked up in a coffin."

"I'm thinking about Mary and Julia. They were quite upset when no one knew where you had gone. You should be in Lexington."

"It doesn't matter. Uncle Thomas is dead."

"It does matter. His wife and child are still alive. You know he would want you there for them."

Sarah had gripped the cloth of Malcolm's uniform tightly in her fingers. "He said he would be in heaven. And here the rest of us are on earth. And we have to live the life of earth."

Malcolm saw her jaw tighten under her skin.

Almost pushing him away she got to her feet.

"Get me to the train, please," she said. "I can only pray to God something good comes out of all this pain and sacrifice."

"I'll pray with you, Sarah. Your uncle gave his life for a new country and this victory puts us one big step closer to what he longed for."

"I should like him to look down and see that. I don't know if he can but I like the idea of him seeing the fulfillment of all his desires."

She hugged Malcolm's arm as they walked.

"Perhaps it is granted," he said. "We don't know. No one knows. But perhaps it is something God blesses the holy dead with."

"I'd like to think so." Her grip on his arm tightened. "What a blessing to think so."

But by the end of the summer Sarah was no longer sure what sort of blessing it would be to her uncle to gaze down from heaven and see what had transpired since he left the earth. The defeat at Gettysburg in July had been difficult for her and the South to take in and it had been compounded by the criticism of Jeb Stuart and his cavalry in the Southern papers – *Why wasn't Jeb Stuart at Gettysburg? Where had he gone with his men? Why did he leave behind his worst officers to fight alongside Lee at such an important engagement?* For Sarah, every criticism of Stuart was a dagger to the heart for she felt it was a criticism of her young husband Malcolm as well.

"No one wants to lay the blame at Lee's feet," Malcolm's father had grumbled, "even though he's the one who sent General Stuart out and planned all the attacks at Gettysburg. So Stuart and his men are the scapegoats."

A Confederate victory at Chickamauga Creek in Georgia in the fall gave her a new burst of hope but that evaporated quickly with defeats at Lookout Mountain and Missionary Ridge near Chattanooga two months later. She did not see Malcolm at Christmas and 1864 seemed to her to be a year of disaster. The Union army under General Grant pushed General Lee and his men farther and farther south towards Richmond, one engagement and brutal battle after another. The day after the anniversary of her uncle's death, on May 11th, Jeb Stuart was mortally wounded at the Battle of Yellow Tavern, six miles north of the Confederate capital, and died on the 12th. Sarah sank down on the porch when the news was brought to her. Even as she grieved Jeb Stuart she asked about her husband. Was there any news of Malcolm Beckett Ross? No news, if he was a casualty his name would appear in the papers. She scanned the newspapers for days after the Yellow Tavern fight, a clash that pitted Confederate cavalry against Union cavalry, reading the long lists of names. Malcolm's name never appeared.

But that means nothing. The newspapers get so much wrong.

A letter from her husband finally made its way to her in June. The constant fighting and constant riding was fierce. Not a day went by that he didn't miss her. Not a day went by that his heart didn't feel cut in two at Jeb's death. He hoped he would be able to stop by Seven Oaks in July. But he never came. What did come in September was the fall of Atlanta, the re-election of Abraham Lincoln in the North in November, and Union General William Tecumseh Sherman's march through Georgia in November and December that destroyed much and left little except the prospect that her country had died.

My God, what are you permitting? Why are you letting our nation crumble to pieces? Why must it burn up and turn into ashes? All our dreams are defeated, all our hopes crushed. I don't understand. What was our sin?

She sat alone on Christmas Day, refusing to go to her in-laws, claiming illness, a plate in front of her with a bit of corn on it, a slice of salted pork, an orange mound of sweet potato. She hardly touched it. Her servants tried to attend her, worried, begging her to eat, but she waved them off.

I will do penance. Will that help our nation, Almighty God? If I fast and pray? If I rend my garments? Will you look on us with favor once again like you did in the first years of the war?

In her room on Christmas night she wrote in her diary: *Nothing has gone right since my uncle died, nothing. That was the beginning of our end. It makes no sense to me. Chancellorsville was the last victory that meant anything and he died to give it to us. But the victory took us nowhere, only to Gettysburg, to Yellow Tavern, to Atlanta. We are a body on a cot just as he was. Our limbs are being amputated, one after another, just as his arm was cut away and buried. We are dead. God alone knows what the North will do with us, with all of us. What do you do with a corpse except dispose of it?*

There were no letters from Malcolm in January or February or March. The Union army broke through into Petersburg in April where Lee's troops had been entrenched since June of 1864. A week later Lee surrendered to Grant at Appomattox. Two weeks on, General Joseph E. Johnston surrendered one hundred thousand soldiers to General Sherman in Durham, North Carolina. Between one surrender and the next, Abraham Lincoln was murdered in Washington. The surrenders and the killing made Sarah sick to her stomach. A neighbor told her Lee had reportedly said the South had lost her best friend.

"He wanted to make us one nation again without penalty or cruelty," the neighbor, Mrs. Kincaid, told her over tea in the parlor. "I know we don't wish to be one nation again but at least he would have made it as painless as possible. That, at least, is General Lee's opinion. Now we shall never know."

"No," Sarah kept her eyes on the cup in her hand.

"The South is not a nation of assassins. What would your uncle have thought?"

"My uncle would not have approved of shooting an unarmed man in the back," Sarah murmured, her eyes still down.

"Exactly, he would not. None of our brave soldiers would." Mrs. Kincaid nibbled at a biscuit. "You can be sure the rest of the North will not be so well disposed towards us as Lincoln. Certainly not after this murder. Heaven knows what they will do to our cities and plantations. I wouldn't be surprised if they burn them down around our ears just as they did Atlanta."

"I hope not."

"Hope, hope, well, we have all of us seen a great number of our hopes dashed. Think of how promising it felt two years ago in the spring of 1863. Do you remember? The splendid victories at Fredericksburg and Chancellorsville, your uncle still in command, our independence just within reach." She extended her hand and snatched at the air in front of her with her fingers. "We almost had it; we almost had it then."

Sarah looked at a spot on the wall over Mrs. Kincaid's right shoulder. "Yes."

"There's nothing we can do to change the past. God's will be done. All we have at our disposal now is prayer. It must suffice." Mrs. Kincaid poured more tea, the steam rising over her white hands. "Let us move onto other topics. Have you heard from your husband, my dear? It's been almost a month since General Lee's surrender."

"No. Nothing yet. No letters, no cables, no news."

"He will be here soon. Depend on it. Grant let Lee's cavalry keep their horses and side arms. He is on his way."

"It is not so long a ride from Appomattox to Seven Oaks, Mrs. Kincaid. It shouldn't take weeks."

"But there is much to do when an army disbands, the officers must do all they can to help their men, he will be here once he is free of his responsibilities, rest easy in that knowledge, your husband will be here in short order." She spooned a dark sugar into her tea. "How did you come by sugar?"

"Billy King found a sack in a corner of the stables. Papa kept it there to treat the horses. I'd completely forgotten about it."

"And the mice didn't get into it?"

"It was in a strong wooden box with iron bands. I think it was an old sea chest."

"Ah." Mrs. Kincaid stirred slowly. Now it was she who kept her eyes down as she swirled the sugar into the tea with her spoon. "Have you not had any news of your brothers?"

"I'm afraid not."

"Nothing in the newspapers, are you sure?"

"I go over the lists of casualties with a magnifying glass, trust me."

The spoon clicked against the sides of the English china cup.

"A homecoming is on its way. We'll pray to that end, my dear. God will not leave you without a husband or brothers. He will not go so far."

"I hope you are right, Mrs. Kincaid."

"Of course I am right. The South may have lost the war but we did not lose our God."

Despite the older woman's assurances the days dragged on without any sign of Malcolm's return or that of her brothers Warren, Christopher, or Samuel. The papers told Sarah nothing and no letters arrived in the mail. The house had been empty for much of the war, and the plantation unusually quiet after the first Union raids in 1861, but Sarah had not let it trouble her – there had been so many victories to celebrate, and her wedding on Valentine's Day in 1863, and the gatherings of the generals and their wives at her table that the weeks had not seemed dreary or lifeless. Now she heard the creaking of every wall or gable in the wind, the groan of every floorboard, the clatter of rainstorms against the roof and panes of glass and she felt smaller and weaker because of it. She fought back by riding over the plantation every morning and walking out among the fields. They had begun to grow tobacco and she was determined to see it become a successful crop that brought much-needed cash back to the estate.

"Are you all right, Miz Sarah?" asked Billy King whenever she climbed down from her mare to examine the rows of tobacco plants.

"I'm perfectly fine, Billy King, just as I was yesterday, and the day before, and just as I'll be tomorrow."

"Y'all don't need to ride out here every day. The tobacco is coming along good."

"I want to see that for myself."

"I'll give you a report each and every evening if you wants."

"I have a good horse and two strong legs and my eyes can still see a country mile. I don't need a report."

"But Miz Sarah – "

"I don't need a report, Billy King."

The nights were long, the house seemed to close in around her like a hood, and sleep didn't come soon enough, or when it did come it never brought peace but dreams that exhausted her, dreams of her parents, of her brothers, of Uncle Thomas. Dreams of Malcolm. Night tortured her so that she sat up by her vanity with cups of a poor coffee made of a few beans and scraps of this and that, hoping it would keep her awake until she collapsed into a sleep that was as deep as falling into a pit. But there were never such sleeps as that for her. As much as she tried to tire herself out that so that her imagination could not fill her head with images of love and joy that were like sword thrusts, her mind always found a way to rend her sleep in two and spill the unwanted faces and smiles into her dreams.

She had lived several lives in the quiet house and she lived them again and again whether she was awake or covered with her sheets and blankets. Each life took something from her. She was twelve with her uncle, fourteen, eighteen and waltzing, but when she sat up abruptly in the night there was nothing with her but her servants and acres of tobacco and great old oak trees leaning over her head and heart.

God help me. God deliver me. God do not abandon me; don't turn your back on me.

In late July she was sitting at the vanity and staring into the mirror and wondering if there was any beauty left in her, anything that her husband or any man might admire, and she heard the house moving in the night with a strong wind, heard the footsteps of her servants, heard the call of birds in the trees near her open window.

The sound of a horse walking was distinct from everything else.

She thought of her father-in-law. But he always drove a carriage.

A courier? From the army? This late? The war was long over, the last Confederate troops had surrendered in June, military couriers would not be making their way over the roadways at midnight anymore.

She went to the window but she could not spot anything even though she could still hear the regular fall of a horse's hooves.

A robe wrapped around her, she descended the staircase in her bare feet.

Billy King had opened the door, a lantern in his hand.

"What is it?" she demanded. "Who is there? Is it a soldier? A messenger?"

He did not respond and she brushed past him.

Malcolm was leading a horse up the drive to the house.

He stopped and stared when he saw the lantern lighting up his wife's face.

"He's lame." Malcolm remained where he was. "I haven't ridden him for the past five miles."

Sarah grasped the lantern and walked down the steps to him. She took in his beard, the long cut on one cheek, the rips and tears in his uniform, the dust, the absence of his sash and slouch hat, the dark tangle of his hair.

He smiled a crooked smile. "I guess I don't look like much."

Her eyes continued to sweep over him. "You look like heaven."

She thrust the lantern out to one side and threw her other arm around him, her lips on his mouth, her fingers clawing at the back of his uniform as if she were dying, cries coming from her throat through the kiss, tears cutting over her cheeks and down over her neck.

"Malcolm, I was frightened."

He dropped his horse's reins and lifted her off the ground, pulling her scent into his lungs, her hair unraveling and covering his face, his hands gripping her like iron. It hurt but she didn't say a thing; it was a good pain and a far better pain than she had been enduring since the death of her uncle at Chancellorsville. Someone took the lantern from her outstretched hand, she scarcely noticed it, but freed up, her hand joined the other on Malcolm's back with just as much spirit, her nails digging into the cloth of his gray tunic as he continued to hold her off the ground so that not even her toes trailed in the dust.

"I love you," he said as they kissed, "I love you and I'm not going anywhere, not for a long time, not for a long, long time."

"Not ever. You won't go anyplace, Malcolm Beckett Ross, certainly not without me, not in a hundred years. You're not getting out of my sight again. Whenever someone gets out of my sight I lose them."

"You're all right? You're all right here? There's been no damage?"

"Sherman didn't march through Virginia like he did Georgia. The last two years were lean but there weren't that many mouths to feed."

"Your brothers. Warren and Samuel and Chris. Are they here?"

"They haven't returned."

Shadows came into Malcolm's eyes. He held off his kisses and lowered her to the ground.

"Sarah, there's still plenty of time."

She shook her head and smiled, the tears on her cheeks. "No, my love, it's been almost four months."

"Soldiers are getting out of prison camps. They're getting out of hospitals. I swear. I saw them on roads and woodland paths from here to Appomattox. From here to Atlanta – yes, I've been to Atlanta and you wouldn't believe it. In one year they've rebuilt so much, streets, houses, parks, it's coming back from the dead. And so are we, Sarah."

"Are we? The South is devastated."

"So was Atlanta. But not anymore. And as Atlanta goes, so goes the South."

She half-laughed. "Is that what you think?"

"We're going to start afresh. All of us. Here at Seven Oaks. At my parents' plantation. In Richmond. Vicksburg. Right across our country – even if it is yoked up to that northern nation again. It's going to be our country and it's going to be different than what the Yankees have, a lot different." He grinned and hugged her. "One nation under God – Virginia and the South."

Now her laugh was full. "You're like a shot of the best brandy in the house. I really believe you could rebuild the Confederacy."

His hands were on both sides of her face. "But not tonight."

Billy King stood on the porch with the lantern he'd taken from Sarah's hand. "Master Malcolm. There is a fresh set of clothes laid out for you for the morning, sir. For now we thought you might wish for your robe and we have laid it on your bed."

Malcolm smiled. "Why, thank you, Billy King, that is most agreeable."

"Welcome home, Major. I thank God you have survived. I praise the good Lord Jesus."

"Thank you again. This is the best homecoming any soldier could hope for."

Sarah placed a hand on his chest. "I should like to escort you to your room and help you on with your robe, my heart. But your parents must know. We can't leave them in agony a moment longer."

"Don't worry. I paid a boy a Yankee dollar to take a note to my mother and father an hour ago. Met him on the road with a fishing pole over his shoulder."

"An hour!" Sarah clamped her hands to her hair and then to her nightgown. "Why, they could be here any moment!"

"They won't be here. I explained that we newlyweds needed time alone. I invited them to dine at Seven Oaks tomorrow at eight – or is it tomorrow already?"

"It is." Sarah laughed. "Oh, it must be. I never retire until well after midnight. I haven't been sleeping that well."

"No? We shall have to change that. My dear, I promise you tonight, this morning, shall be such an historic event and so drain the restless spirits from you that you shall sleep like Stone Mountain of Georgia."

"Is that part of your plan for rebuilding the South?"

"It is. And I can tell you it is of the highest priority."

She slid her arm through his. "I shall do everything in my power to see that your plan is completed."

"Excellent."

As they mounted the steps to the porch together, Malcolm nodded to Billy King. "We should not be disturbed on any account. Not even if William Tecumseh Sherman shows up at the gates."

Billy King smiled. "We don't want no Tecumseh Sherman 'round here, sir. If he shows his face we'll give him the bayonet."

"That's the spirit."

"Good night, sir. Good night, Miz Sarah."

"Thank you, Billy King. No breakfast. Lunch at noon will be fine."

Billy King followed them into the mansion with the lantern. "Just as you say, Miz Sarah."

In ten minutes the entire house was dark.

And Malcolm was right. If Stone Mountain of Georgia slept, Sarah slept like that mountain that morning and right until the stroke of noon.

From that time forward Sarah lived in the present and no longer in the past. The days she could not return to but which she relived in her dreams disappeared from her nights and were replaced by images of light or colors of green or dark blue that slid in and out of each other and filled her with peace. By day the tobacco grew and ripened and was finally hung in a long barn that used to hold cattle and now was used for curing the tobacco leaves with a small fire that smoldered for days at a time. By night she and Malcolm became the heart of Seven Oaks, giving new life not only to the plantation and its crops and the mansion but to the servants who had remained with Sarah as well. As the days sharpened and the rains fell onto the leaves of October and November they opened their doors to their neighbors, a number of who were struggling in the months following the Southern defeat.

"I had gold put aside of course," said Jacob Marsh in the library with Malcolm and the other men. "As much as I believed in the Confederacy I could not place great faith in their paper notes. But in order to keep our plantation afloat since the fall of Atlanta and

Lincoln's re-election and Appomattox I have had to use it all. We are barely scarping by. It's a bitter pill and I refuse to accept Yankee aid."

"I don't blame you," responded Malcolm, "but are you willing to accept loans from Southerners?"

"What? Banks? They are in a mess too. And they are liable to take my estate if I default."

"Never mind banks and bankers. The New South must pull together. What we lost on the battlefield we shall regain by our industry and economy and community. No plantation in our district should fail. We must stand shoulder to shoulder."

"What did you have in mind, sir?" Marsh asked.

"Let us meet for coffee in the morning, you and I, and discuss it. We must keep Virginia intact."

By December of 1865 many parts of the South rumbled with discontent as Federal troops in blue marched up and down the streets and Washington's iron rule of Reconstruction tightened around thousands of Southern men's throats. It was not so in the county where Seven Oaks thrived due to tobacco and pork sales. Sarah and Malcolm gave cash loans in Yankee dollars to several neighbors, including Jacob and Marietta Marsh, and other plantation owners followed suit, assisting struggling friends by whatever means they could – food, money, livestock.

"Still we can do more, Malcolm," Sarah said one evening as they sat by the fire in the library.

Malcolm was smoking his churchwarden pipe with its foot long stem. "What more? It will take time but we shall all get back on our feet again."

Her large family Bible was open on her lap. "For their souls we can do more."

"The church services are full. The minister is a good man."

"Yes, of course. But suppose we asked Mary Jackson and Julia up? Flora Stuart as well and she must bring young James, he's five, and little Virginia who turned two in October. And General Lee and his wife and any of their children who wish to join us here."

"Why, suppose they can all gather here. You couldn't do it right on Christmas Day, General Lee would wish to be in Richmond and –"

"The week before. That's good enough. Haven't you told me a thousand times the Lord wasn't born on December 25th anyways?

We shall invite our neighbors and set a splendid table in the ballroom."

"What? And dance too?"

"I don't know; I don't know, so many hearts are still like lead after the calamity of Appomattox, a dance wouldn't hurt, but I just wish to get invitations out tomorrow so everyone can make plans."

"The widows may beg off."

"I shall implore them, Malcolm. We had such blessings here during the war. Why may we not have further blessings during a season of peace?"

"Because we had more peace during the war. While your uncle and Jeb were still alive we won every battle we turned our hand to and that gave us all great joy. There are no victories now except what we are gaining by pulling ourselves up by the bootstraps."

"The same God who was with us then is with us now. Did David turn away when there were defeats? He cried out to God even more. Isn't that what we're supposed to do? Use our struggles and sufferings and losses as vehicles that convey us towards the Lord rather than away from him?"

Malcolm drew on his pipe until the ashes in the bowl glowed red. "Sound theology, my dear. But as it is with so much theology far easier to discuss by a warm fire or write down on paper in a warm study than to live out under gloomy skies of heavy rain or on land that is hardened by bitter frost."

"David's faith wasn't lived out by fireplaces or in warm rooms when his world had fallen apart. Often enough he was in hiding or on the run or bereft of food and comfort. Often enough he did not feel God's presence. But he looked to him all the same. Just as I did when I never knew if you were dead or alive. *My God, my God,* I cried out. I was in so much pain. Just as all Virginia and the South are now. I've lost both parents and all my brothers. But I continue to take my agony to him. Where else shall I take it? Who else can assuage it? Who else is divine enough to succor me when it comes to such matters of life and death? Who else deals in eternity and immortality and redemption and the saving graces of our Savior Jesus Christ? So we must have a holy gathering here at Seven Oaks as we pause to not only remember our Redeemer's birth but to remember he was given to us as light in darkness, hope when things were hopeless, salvation when all around was damnation. We must make this Christmas of 1865 a Christmas of turning our faces to God as much or more than we ever have before. My uncle would have wanted us to do this; I know it. And I cannot believe General Lee will not feel the same way."

Malcolm stared at her during her outburst. Finally he laughed. "You get a few minutes with your Bible and a world that is turned upside down is for a little while turned right side up." He set aside his pipe and got up out of his chair. Leaning over her he kissed her on the cheek. Then he headed for the door.

"Where are you going?" she asked.

"To fetch our best paper and our best pens. If you will trust my scrawl we shall get the invitations out tomorrow morning. After that it is in the hands of God whether there shall be feast or famine at Seven Oaks this Christmas. But from the sounds of it that is where you wish the matter to rest in any case."

She smiled. "I do."

"So we will endeavor to turn our faces and our neighbors' faces towards the Lord God during this hard Christmas. And see if Robert E. Lee cannot help us win this battle of turning the South's hearts to God as he helped us win so many other battles at the height of our nation's glory."

"It is a victory if we can bless our people in this way, Malcolm, a victory as great as any other. Perhaps we may even be an example to the Yankees."

"The Yankees!"

"They have their own burdens to bear and they too have lost many sons and brothers on the battlefield. They need God as much as we do and God will not spurn any who come to him. Aren't many of them our brothers and sisters in Christ? We talk about the South. But we are joined together again. We want God to bless all of us. Not just Virginia and the Confederate states."

Malcolm remained standing in the doorway. "I hear you, my love. But your heart is bigger than many other hearts in the South right now. Pray that way. But speak what our friends can understand for the moment and what they can grasp. God is great in his grace and compassion and you do not seem to be far behind him. But the rest of us are very far back on the heavenly road this Christmas, I fear."

"It may not be that way after our banquet at Seven Oaks."

He nodded. "Indeed it may not. Especially if Sarah's prayers and petitions to the Almighty have anything to do with it." He tapped the doorframe with his fingers. "Now I shall do something to speed your hopes on their way. Fetch paper and pens."

Sarah glanced at the Bible in her lap.

But God, who is rich in mercy, for his great love wherewith he loved us,

Even when we were dead in sins, hath quickened us together with Christ, (by grace ye are saved;)

And hath raised us up together, and made us sit together in heavenly places in Christ Jesus:

That in the ages to come he might shew the exceeding riches of his grace in his kindness toward us through Christ Jesus.

For by grace are ye saved through faith; and that not of yourselves: it is the gift of God.

"In the ages to come you will show all of us the exceeding riches of your grace," she said out loud. "Not just a handful. All of us, North and South. For that is the gift. That is the kindness through Christ Jesus. That is Christmas." She closed her eyes. "Fill our ballroom and fill our hearts. In these hard times, show us what matters the most. But not just this dark year, my God. In all the years to come whether they are grim or glorious. Don't let us lose sight of you. Not ever." Her fingers brushed at her eyes. "That is what my uncle would have said. That is what he would have told us if he'd lived and had to suffer through this defeat. Ultimately we cannot be saved by force of arms but only by you, our Lord. That is the gift we cannot buy with all the Yankee gold in Washington; that is the salvation we cannot earn with all the sweat of our brow. Only you can bestow it. Only you can place it in our hearts in the midst of our greatest failures and greatest losses. *Although the fig tree shall not blossom, neither shall fruit be in the vines; the labor of the olive shall fail, and the fields shall yield no meat; the flock shall be cut off from the fold, and there shall be no herd in the stalls: Yet I will rejoice in the LORD, I will joy in the God of my salvation.*" Her soft crying dropped onto the Bible pages, wetting and wrinkling them. "You loved those verses. You quoted them to me time after time. Thank you, uncle. It's your own gift to me during this difficult winter for our people. A God who did not fail you in your own death but took you across the river to the shade trees. A God who will not fail us as we cross our own river and seek beauty and peace on the other side. You know all this better than I do now, Uncle Thomas, for you are with the angels. Angels? You are with our Savior himself. *Unto you is born this day in the city of David a Savior who is Christ the Lord."*

Slowly she shut her Bible.

"Merry Christmas, Uncle Thomas. If you can look down wish us well here at Seven Oaks. I hope they will come; I so hope all our old friends will come and bring good cheer to the people near us."

And they did come that week before Christmas Day 1865. Jeb Stuart's widow Flora and her children, Stonewall Jackson's widow Mary and her daughter Julia, General Lee and his wife and three of their grown girls, sitting at table again, remembering for a time how they had laughed and toasted and waltzed at Seven Oaks when all had been well and Jeb and Stonewall had been with them. At first Sarah could not drive off the pall that descended on the group at the head table. But after neighbors joined them in the ballroom and sat at the other tables around the vast room, General Lee seemed to come to himself and asked if he would be permitted to read the Christmas story from Luke out loud to the gathering. He concluded with a short prayer of thanks for the meal and wished everyone a Merry Christmas. This seemed to break any spell of gloom. The servants brought the platters of meat and sweet potato up and all the guests dug in with a feeling of hope. For there was Lee, bearing up under the defeat, praising his God and Savior, and placing his faith above everything else, above his disappointments, above the loss of personal friends and generals like Stuart and Jackson, and above any regrets he still wrestled with from engagements like Gettysburg and Appomattox. If Lee could rise again so could they. If he could look towards God in such times so could they. If he and the widows at his table could believe when they had lost so many of those they loved, just as many in the room had, so could they.

"Will there be carols?" Lee looked at Malcolm. "Shall someone lead out with carols once the meal is finished?"

"Why, I had not thought of it, sir." Malcolm looked from General Lee to his wife and the two widows. "Does the prospect of caroling appeal to everyone at the table?"

"I should rather sing a few carols and hymns than not." Flora Stuart did not smile but light came into her eyes. "Jeb would have sung louder than cannon fire."

Mary Jackson and Sarah laughed at the same time when Flora said this.

"Well, if Jeb was cannon fire then my husband would have been the rebel yell when it came to carols," Mary said. "It would not have been so tuneful perhaps but he would have made up in spirit what he lacked in melody. By all means sing. God asks us to do it and heaven knows the people need food for their souls as much as they need it for their bodies."

Malcolm bowed his head. "It shall be so. Would you like to begin the singing, General Lee?"

Lee held up his hand. "I shall be fifty-nine in January. Let someone else begin and I shall join the charge. But a younger voice ought to lead the way. Such as yours, Major."

"I would be honored, sir. Is there a carol the General particularly favors?"

"Let us begin with *O Come All Ye Faithful*. That is what Southerners have always been with regards to our Lord. That is what we must remain throughout all the vicissitudes and vagaries of life. Pray sing out with all your heart and strength, Major, and I know the people here assembled will join in most heartily in return."

"I will endeavor to do that, General." Malcolm rose to his feet. "My Christian friends and neighbors, it would please the General and the ladies at the head table if we completed our meal with some food for the spirit. It is Christmas, perhaps the hardest Christmas the South has ever known, but our God is faithful and we are called upon to be faithful in return. Will you join me in singing *O Come All Ye Faithful?*"

Murmurs of assent and a clapping of hands swept the room.

Malcolm began.

O come all ye faithful, joyful and triumphant
O come ye, O come ye to Bethlehem
Come and behold him, born the King of angels

At the chorus the entire room joined him.

O come let us adore him
O come let us adore him
O come let us adore him
Christ the Lord

Sarah turned from watching General Lee and the ladies and children to look out at the faces in the ballroom. Everyone was singing when her husband began the second verse.

True God of true God, Light from Light Eternal
Lo, he shuns not the Virgin's womb

Son of the Father, begotten not created

She closed her eyes and stopped singing so that she could better take in the thunder of the male voices and the sweet strength of the higher voices of the women.

This will be our future if we wish it. This will carry us through all our days, whatever those days may bring, if only we are as faithful in following God, despite all circumstances, as he is faithful in tending to us, despite all circumstances. Here we are, Uncle Thomas. We are going forward again just as you would have us do. Forward into battle. A different kind of battle but one that you knew as well as those where swords clashed and muskets blazed. A battle of the heart. We shall win it. We shall all of us win it. So help me God.

"Glory to God in the highest," she seemed to hear her uncle rumble at her side. "It is painful enough to discover with what unconcern they speak of war and threaten it. They do not know its horrors. I have seen enough of it to make me look upon it as the sum of all evils."

Sarah turned as if he were seated next to her at the table. "Glory to God in the highest. And on earth peace, good will towards men."

Despite his thick beard, she imagined his lips forming into a satisfied smile and the smile was in the quiet blue of his eyes as well.